The Stars that Fell

By

M.L. Bullock

This book is dedicated to Lula Mae, a true Southern lady—strong, gentle and always believing the best in all those you love.

Though my soul may set in darkness, it will rise in perfect light;
I have loved the stars too fondly to be fearful of the night.

—Sarah Williams, 1868

Prologue

Mobile, Alabama, 1851

Hoyt Page never wanted to become a physician, but his family's good name required him to take up a respectable occupation. Since he loathed the prospect of a lifetime of military service or the pretense of local politics, medicine appeared his only option. To his and his family's surprise, he excelled at his craft.

Generally, Hoyt did not care to engage people in conversation unless the topic touched on a subject he held an interest in, like astronomy or pedigree horses. Too many times, he stood awkwardly through sessions of idle chitchat only to excuse himself before he made the unforgiveable mistake of yawning. However, people in pain—that was quite another story. Those he could speak with all day, listening to their list of symptoms, offering comfort and wisdom. Hoyt found he had a mile-wide streak of compassion for the sick and infirm. He himself was a healthy man and had been a healthy child, but his concern for the sick was real and nothing he intentionally cultivated. Hoyt was committed to his work and did not mind the midnight calls, the long rides and the bone-aching weariness. Even those terrifying moments when he left a home feeling powerless to heal—yes, even in those moments, he knew he was walking in his unique purpose.

Just like tonight. He left Seven Sisters with his stiff black hat in his hands, his bag feeling unusually heavy. Every step he took away from the mansion brought him both relief and extreme regret. Jeremiah Cottonwood was an evil, reprehensible man, probably the angriest man Hoyt had ever known. Even Hoyt's father's temperament could not compare to Cottonwood's. The man married Christine Beaumont, the most beautiful woman in the state, but had that satisfied the arrogant bastard? Had her wealth and quiet beauty calmed his rambunctious spirit? No, of course not. Jeremiah Cottonwood had used her with hopes of getting a son—the son he needed to maintain control of his wife's extraordinary wealth. Hoyt's own cynicism surprised him. He shuddered and stoked the fire, which had died hours ago in his absence.

How many times had Hoyt visited the sheriff to voice his concerns over the treatment of Christine and her daughter Calpurnia? At least four now, but nothing had changed. What could he do? With a grimace, he recalled the conversation he'd just had with the sheriff of Mobile.

"Come now, Dr. Page. You should leave the gossip to the ladies. It's not seemly for a man in your position to engage in this kind of speculation," Sheriff Rice had said as his deputy and oldest son had snickered and leaned back on his dirty boot heels. Hoyt had cast a glance at the deputy over his shoulder but continued undaunted, determined to help Christine. "Do you have any proof that Mr. Cottonwood has abused either of them?" the sheriff had asked.

"What kind of proof do you need, sir? I know starvation when I see it. The girl is nothing but skin and bones, and her skin is sallow—both obvious signs of starvation. Her mother can't even speak—she's catatonic, unable to do anything by herself. Something is going on in that house."

"Did they complain to you, doctor?"

"No," Hoyt had said with a surge of desperation, "but I want it on record as the family's physician that I made a formal complaint. I cannot sit idly by while the man starves his daughter to death. God only knows what Christine—Mrs. Cottonwood—has had to endure. Have you ever known me to gossip about a patient or any family that I have cared for? Won't you at least investigate what I am reporting?"

"Surely you understand how sensitive this type of matter is, Dr. Page." Rice had stroked his greasy black beard like it was his favorite cat. His dark eyes were steady and fierce; they seemed to bore into Hoyt's soul. Hoyt had been unnerved that he couldn't read him.

"I am not asking you to arrest anyone. Just investigate. Please, sheriff. I would consider this a personal favor." Hoyt understood what that meant. The next time another fool deputy shot his toe or another one of Rice's relatives developed syphilis, Hoyt would offer his care for free—until Rice said otherwise. *No matter. It is worth it if it helps Christine!*

Sheriff Rice's wooden chair had squeaked as he'd sprung to his feet and offered Hoyt his hand. Hoyt had shook it tentatively and thanked him. "If it will ease your mind, Dr. Page, I will do it. If I see any cause to intervene, I will. You have my word."

With a nod, Hoyt had left the office, hoping to make it home before the rain began to fall. That was earlier that evening—it was now near midnight. It was a fortunate thing that the sheriff had been in his office. He had felt hopeful at first, but it hadn't lasted.

Knowing the sheriff's character, it was doubtful that Christine, Calpurnia and now the new baby would receive any help at all. He sat at his writing desk, wondering to whom he should write—who would help him? There was a judge, Judge Klein, who used to serve as a circuit judge. But what influence would he have here now? He sighed again and reached for the small cedar box hidden in the secret drawer of his desk. Not even his sister knew of his personal treasure trove.

Dearest Dr. Page,

Against the desires of my own heart, I have consented to marry Jeremiah Cottonwood. As this pleases my parents, it also pleases me. Had my father not suffered so extreme a shame at the hands of my sister, Olivia, I may have better resisted his pleas. Olivia has brought a cloud upon our name, and I dare not speak her name in public, not in the presence of a living soul.

Even Louis agrees that my marriage to Mr. Cottonwood is the wisest course of action for our family, although he continues to respect and admire your noble character. Truthfully, he does not express much care for my intended but assures me that he will remain by my side to guide me in my new role as the lady of Seven Sisters.

My friend (I call you this because you are still my dear friend despite this troubling news), you cannot imagine how unhappy I am at the possibility that I will no longer receive your Kind and Enjoyable Favor.

Please forgive me,
C.B.

He had not written back. In fact, it had been a full year before he saw her again. It had been at the Ferguson-Mays Christmas Ball at the Idlewood Mansion. He closed his eyes and remembered that night. The Greek revival home had been full of Mobile's elite....

***

Fragrant greenery decorated the balustrades and mantelpieces, and white and red candles flickered everywhere. The dark wooden panels of the parlor gleamed, and even the servants wore fine cuffs and tails.

Snow fell for the first time in a decade, and the gentlefolk spent a great deal of time gathered at the massive windows, watching the sparkling snow and dancing flakes in the comfort and warmth of the mansion. Two young cocker spaniels leaped up on the back of one of the couches and began barking excitedly. The partiers laughed at the entertainment, and this was the scene to which he entered. With the recent surge of influenza and other illnesses, it was a welcome picture of joy that he rarely witnessed. He handed his hat and coat to a servant and politely nodded to those who greeted him.

Immediately, his eyes fell upon Christine. Her dark blond hair no longer hung prettily down her back in carefully combed tendrils; instead she wore it in an elegant swirl at the back of her head, as a respectable married woman would. Delicate pearls dangled from her pretty ears, and she wore an expensive dark red dress. Some women could not wear such a shade without looking pale, but Christine's beautiful shoulders and bright skin made her look like a crimson angel. Hoyt drew himself up straight, suddenly proud of his height—he was well over six feet and easily one of the tallest men in the room. Although he was thirty, he maintained a trim physique and a healthy metabolism. Some women found him attractive, he gathered, but he considered his brown hair and hazel eyes rather plain.

Hoyt stared—he could not help himself. That he had thus far managed to avoid socializing with Christine had been nothing short of sheer luck. Now that he stood so close, he felt his heart melt. Yes, she had chosen Jeremiah Cottonwood over him, but how could he blame her? She, the obedient daughter of the Beaumonts, could do nothing but obey her father's wishes. Strangely enough, that made Hoyt love her more. Her sense of duty was as fierce as his own. All this time, he had asked himself if he had really loved her, and now he knew the answer. Indeed he had, and he loved her still.

Hoyt silently prayed that Christine would look in his direction, but she was engrossed in a conversation with one of the Maples twins. The hostess of the ball, Margaret Ferguson, suddenly stepped into his line of sight. "I am so happy to see you, Dr. Page. It has been far too long since you stepped foot in Idlewood. How long must it be? Two years? And how is your sister? Still not well? I miss my friend."

Returning Mrs. Ferguson's smile, Hoyt offered Claudette's formal apologies. "Alas, Mrs. Ferguson, she hasn't the strength right now for a night of dancing. But I feel sure another few weeks will have her right as rain. She asks that you excuse her just this once, and she promises she will return to your side in time for the church auction in January."

Her smile deepened, and she gave him a courteous nod. "Of course I excuse her, poor thing. This year's flu has wreaked havoc here too. Almost all my servants have succumbed to it, and now our boy is sick...."

"I pray it leaves your household soon, ma'am." Suddenly, he could hear the swell of violins and the sliding of the wooden panels that transformed the front parlors into a spacious ballroom.

Mrs. Ferguson leaned toward him and whispered, "Would it be vile of me to ask you to check on my Charles before you leave? My husband does not trust physicians, I am afraid; however, I would value your opinion. I cannot imagine what I would do if..." She sniffled as she confessed her greatest fear to him.

"I will be happy to examine the boy, but I am afraid I left my bag in my coach."

Her nervous smile reappeared. "I will ask Daniel to bring the bag up to you. Would it be possible for you to visit Charles now? That way my husband will not suspect anything. I do not think he knows yet that you are here."

"Of course, as you wish."

"His room is up the stairs, to the right. I will go find Daniel now."

"Leave him in my hands. All will be well."

"Thank you so much, Dr. Page."

Although with all his heart Hoyt wanted to greet Christine, he went up the stairs just as Mrs. Ferguson asked. He walked with his hands clasped behind his back, and his stiff collar felt hot and uncomfortable on his skin. He pushed open one door and found a young black woman busily folding linen. "Excuse me," he whispered as he closed the door behind him and continued to the second door. There was a low lamp lit on a desk in the second room, and Hoyt could discern the shadows of furniture, toys and books. *This must be the nursery*. A light glimmered on the other side of the room, and he could hear a child coughing.

He walked quietly through the nursery to the child's room and noticed a draft. He made a mental note to mention that to Mrs. Ferguson. The boy rolled over in his bed and looked up at him.

"Hello, young sir. You must be Charles. Your mother asked me to come see you. I am a doctor. Would you mind if I took a look at your eyes, nose and ears?"

The child said nothing, but his dark eyes had a shadowy, sickly look. Hoyt's heart went out to the poor little fellow. As he sat on the bed, a young man came into the room with his bag. Absently, Hoyt thanked him and opened the bag, looking for his liniment. He felt the child's head—he had a fever, and a high one. Fevers were child killers. He moved the lamp closer to the child's face and examined his eyes. The pupils were dilated slightly, and his throat felt swollen. "Oh, yes. That hurts, doesn't it?"

The frail boy nodded, and Hoyt continued his examination, peering into the youth's red ears and inspecting his runny nose. Fortunately, the mucus was clear with no obvious signs of infection. Either the boy's case was early in the going or this was not the flu. A sharp knock on the door grabbed the pair's attention. Hoyt stood quickly, wondering what he would say if Lane Ferguson came barging in wondering why Hoyt was examining his son. The door opened and Christine entered, her soft red dress filling the small room with happy color. Hoyt's heart leaped in his chest.

"Who are you?" the boy whispered, his voice sounding scratchy and hoarse.

"Why, I am Christine. I am Dr. Page's nurse."

"You don't look like a nurse, ma'am. You're too pretty to be a nurse."

"How charming you are, sir," she answered with a smile. "How is the patient, doctor?" Her dainty hand grasped the post of the twin bed as she smiled down at him.

Hoyt's mouth was as wide as the child's astonished eyes. He could tell that the young boy was quite infatuated with Christine, but who could blame him? His heart beat fast in his chest, and he felt a smile stretch across his lips. "Our patient will recover as long as he gets plenty of rest and drinks all the soup his mother brings him. Can you do that?"

"Yes, I can do that."

Hoyt stuffed his tools back in his bag, tousled the lad's hair and walked toward the door. What should he do? What should he say now?

"Goodbye, nurse. I hope you come see me again."

"I shall, I promise, young man. Good night." She walked out of the drafty room and Hoyt followed her, his bag in hand. They walked into the nursery, where several tiny lights bounced and shimmered; she must have lit the candles before she entered the bedroom. Swells of music rose from the lower floor, and candlelight sparkled from the greenery-decked mantelpiece. Christine took Hoyt's hand and led him to a tufted couch at the corner of the room.

Hoyt's hands were freezing, and panic gripped him. *Should I take her hand or refrain? Should I...what should I do?* He stared at her, not daring to touch her or ask why she had come upstairs. Just as he summoned the courage to touch her cheek and speak his mind, Christine turned her attention to the window. She made a comment about the snow—how beautiful it was, how quickly it would be gone—but Hoyt barely listened. The small talk made him impatient, and he rose to join her. Standing behind her, he quietly examined her hair, her elegant neck, the milk-white skin of her bosom. None of these had he ever had permission to touch or appreciate. How he'd fantasized about her hair falling through his fingers, her upturned face tilting toward his. Christine spun around, the silk of her dress rustling as she did.

Here was the moment he had been waiting for! He grasped her thin arms, pulling her close to him. He wanted to rail at her, yell at her for leaving him, but he couldn't. Her sweet lips beckoned him and he kissed her, softly, chastely at first, then more ardently.

"What if your husband…" Hoyt couldn't help himself. The unwanted words came tumbling forth.

"No! Do not mention his name! Don't spoil this, Hoyt! Let this moment be for you and me!" The two embraced, uncaring that anyone could enter the room and find them. In a ragged whisper she said, "All I need is this moment. That's all I need. Then I can go on."

There was a message in her confession—a desperation that made Hoyt both protective and angry. He felt it with every inch of his being.

Before he could seek the source of her anxiety, she whispered, "Come to me at four o'clock tomorrow, Hoyt. If you don't come, I don't know how I will make it. I need your strength. You have always been my friend and…even more. Promise me you will come."

"Where shall I meet you?"

"Come to Seven Sisters. Ann-Sheila will lead you to me."

"What of Cottonwood? Won't he be suspicious to see me calling upon you?"

"He leaves in the morning. Tell Stokes you've come to check up on Ann. She's been ill recently. He won't suspect anything."

"I will come, Christine."

"I had better go now, before someone misses me. Until tomorrow." She squeezed his hand and smiled at him.

Hoyt's heart banged happily in his chest as he watched her leave the room. He tried to gather himself, wandering around the room and pretending to be interested in the impressive selection of children's fairy stories on the shelf next to the couch. As patiently as he could, he forced himself to wait. No one must know their intentions. Mobile society was unforgiving when it came to infidelity, but was this truly infidelity? Weren't they meant for one another? Besides, Hoyt knew the secrets of just about all these old families—including his own. After what seemed like a lifetime, he walked out of the room and discreetly passed his bag to Daniel, who took it to his carriage.

Hoyt danced a mere four times, drank two hot whiskeys and discreetly excused himself far earlier than his sister would have liked. The entire night, he did not speak to Christine—it wasn't seemly to dance with a married woman unless she was a cousin or a sister-in-law. He could not bear to think he might bring her scandal or heartache.

Jeremiah Cottonwood greeted him during the course of the evening, preening like a peacock and showing everyone the gold chain and watch his eminent father-in-law had given him. After a few drinks, he began to share bawdy jokes. He was careful not to speak ill of his rich wife, but Hoyt was sure he was tempted to do so. As far as Cottonwood believed, he was the luckiest man in the room—twice as wealthy as anyone there and four times as wealthy as his hosts. But that did not humble the man at all. Hoyt considered it a pleasure to leave his company.

He spent a restless night in his modest two-story brick home, tossing and turning, wishing sleep would come and make the time go faster. The next day, he went out for a haircut and a shave, purchased a new shirt and came back home and watched the grandfather clock move ever so slowly. At three, he saddled up his horse and rode toward Seven Sisters. With any luck, Cottonwood would not be home and Hoyt could spend time with the woman he loved.

Ann-Sheila, Christine's constant companion, greeted him at the door. That was highly unusual, as Stokes was such a fixture there. Hoyt was so surprised that he inquired about Stokes' health, but Ann-Sheila assured him he was well and only away on business for Mr. Cottonwood. He knew her; she had been always present during his attempts to court his beloved. With a perfect smile and natural grace, she welcomed him into the plantation. It was a marvelous place with dark plum settees and plush carpets, the likes of which he had never seen. The only problem—it belonged to Cottonwood. Ann-Sheila led Hoyt to the ladies' parlor and began to give him a list of her false symptoms. Eventually the two were alone and the young woman leaned forward and whispered into his ear. "She's waiting for you in the Rose Garden. Out the side entrance just there."

Unable to wait any longer, Hoyt handed her his hat, bag and riding crop. He scrambled out the French doors, his steps hastening him to his deepest desire. The hedges surrounding the garden grew thick but were well-manicured by obviously talented gardeners. Hoyt had never been in this garden, but his beloved left clues for him along the way. A glove here, a book there, and finally he found her.

She sat under a wisteria-wrapped oak, her pale, perfect hands resting peacefully in her lap. When she spotted him, she rose and ran toward him, her eyes never wavering. "I wasn't sure you would come."

"How could you wonder?"

Her arms went around his neck, and they kissed like they were always meant to—with complete and utter abandon. Finally, when he couldn't stand the tension anymore he asked her, "Where can we go?" Taking him by the hand, Christine led him out of the maze to a sandy, narrow path. He could hear water rushing nearby, perhaps the Mobile River. Hoyt never questioned her; he followed obediently until they were alone in a small white cottage. How hurried they had been, that first time together! That stolen hour had been too brief but so passionate. They didn't talk about Jeremiah; in fact, Hoyt rarely thought about him except for on the few unhappy occasions he had to face him.

The following year, Hoyt had the pleasure of helping Christine bring their child into the world. It was an experience he had never expected, and it moved him deeply. He never doubted that the child was his—Christine confided in him that Cottonwood rarely sought her bed, and when he did his drunkenness made it impossible for him to perform his duty; however, she always left him so that he believed he had done the deed.

* * *

Hoyt took a swig of his brandy—it had been a gift from his sister. How close they used to be. How could he tell her about his secret life? Like their mother, Claudette would die of shame if she knew about his love for Christine. He poured another drink and thought about how wretched his situation had become. That night, he had held another baby; looking down at her sweet face filled him with joy, but even that had not roused Christine. His beloved was unresponsive, even when he whispered to her. Hoyt never claimed the child—that would bring Christine to ruin. But what should he do? He must take action! Surely he must! Regardless of the cost to his reputation or that of his family. But for now, he would wait a little bit longer. There was always hope that Christine would arise from her bed, her mind refreshed. Then what would she say to him?

Hoyt loved Christine as if she were his own wife, as she rightfully should have been. Now, they had delivered another one of their children into this world, only Christine could not see the baby, or Hoyt or anyone she had loved. Ann-Sheila, Christine's faithful friend, had been killed years ago, and since then, his sweetheart had been a broken person. Now here was his child, *their* child, yet he could not claim her. This was a sacrifice he must make—for his beloved and their children.

After Calpurnia was born, he and Christine experienced loss after loss, their children dying after a few days at most. Now tonight, another baby, likely their last, was born. Christine was now catatonic from some unknown, unspoken suffering, obviously at the hands of Cottonwood. If he could get his hands on that bastard just one time, he would show him how it felt. How often he fantasized about killing the man—how easy that would be! Cottonwood was a known drunk, yet he had powerful friends, including the sheriff and a few notable politicians.

With a surge of anger, he sent his glass crashing across the room, the warm liquid streaming down the carefully painted gray wall. Finally he cried, collapsing on his couch, the complete powerlessness overwhelming him at last. It was there where he slept until an urgent rap at the door woke him. He'd been dreaming—something vile, something horrible.

He woke in complete darkness, the fire almost gone and the room as cold as death. He squinted at the grandfather clock, but he couldn't make out the time without his glasses. The knocking continued, and he could hear something else…the sound of a baby crying.

Exhausted but curious, he walked to the front door. It was raining—he could hear fat droplets splashing against the windowpanes in the parlor. Lightning cracked across the sky. Hoyt opened the door and blinked against a nearby burst of bright light. His natural instinct was to insist that the young woman at the door come inside out of the rain, but he could not do so yet. It was illegal to give aid and comfort to a runaway slave, and he couldn't be sure she was here on behalf of her owner. She slid back her cloak so he could see her anguished face. Hoyt could tell that she had been crying, perhaps as much as the baby had.

"What are you doing out here with the baby? With Mrs. Cottonwood's baby? Have you lost your mind?" Then the thought suddenly came to him. *What if she was here because of Christine—what if his love had died?* "Has something happened to Mrs. Cottonwood or Miss Calpurnia?"

"No, sir. I mean, I don't know of anything. I'm here because of the baby."

"What? Why would you bring the baby out in a thunderstorm, Hannah? That's your name, correct?"

"Yes, sir, that's my name." Another pop of lightning lit up the narrow lane. Hannah gasped, and the baby began to cry in earnest. "But I had to come, lightning or no! The master said this baby is dead. You have to take it!" She handed the writhing bundle to him.

Puzzled, Hoyt stared at her. "What? She's alive! I hear her crying! Take her home."

Hannah screamed in agony, "No! No, Dr. Hoyt! Please don't send the baby back. Please listen! Hooney told me to come—the master says this baby is dead."

Still stymied, Hoyt pressed on. "Come inside, Hannah, and warm yourself by the fire. Let's figure out exactly what you are saying."

"No, I can't go in there. Hooney said I was to come right back because Miss Calpurnia would need me. The master told us, 'The baby is dead.' He don't want no dead baby! We was to get rid of it."

Awareness rose like a black sun in Hoyt's mind. Would Cottonwood murder a baby? A baby he believed was his child? Hoyt snatched the bundle away from her in desperation. The baby's cries were now more pitiful and heartbreaking. Crying loudly herself, Hannah ran from Hoyt, no doubt back to Seven Sisters.

Hoyt stood in the doorway as the enveloping darkness swallowed Hannah's tiny figure. She was gone from sight in seconds. He brought his daughter indoors and found a warm blanket to wrap her in. As she cried, Hoyt stoked the fire, his mind working to figure out what he should do next. What did this mean for Christine? If it weren't for the baby, he would have driven the carriage back to Seven Sisters right away—thunderstorm be damned!

Leaving the unhappy baby crying on the settee, Hoyt ran to his neighbor's door and banged on it until she answered. He managed to acquire a pint of milk without giving too many details about why. Mixing a little sugar in the milk so the child would sleep better, he fed his hungry daughter until she fell asleep, satisfied at last. He arranged her on his bed, wrapping her tenderly in the soft blanket. He left her only long enough to raise a warm fire in the bedroom fireplace.

For the first and last time, he slept peacefully beside his child, knowing in his heart that tomorrow he must let her go. He had to protect Christine. Let the world believe the child was dead—he knew that she wasn't. She was beautiful, perfect and alive! As he lay in the dark, smelling her hair and allowing her tiny fingers to wrap around his finger, he cried. At least he had this moment—it was more than he deserved. He prayed for Christine and asked God to forgive him for all their trespasses.

He knew what he had to do. He could not keep his daughter, but he had to take her somewhere safe. No foundling hospital. He remembered the young couple on the other side of the county, the Iversons, who owned a small store. They had lost a baby two weeks ago. Surely, they would welcome a child of their own now. But for now, he held his baby close. Staring at her in the dim light, he could see Christine's perfect bow lips, his own eyes and his beloved's tapered, elegant fingers. He lingered in the moment, knowing it would disappear with the rising of the sun. His life had been unconventional, not at all the way he had envisioned, but it was his. Soon he fell asleep, dreaming of nothing and no one.

Sometime during the night, he felt a draft blow through the room.

He smelled roses, the sweet, large blooms of wild roses that grow only on vines. Those had been Christine's favorite. He must have been dreaming—what a pleasant dream! Hoyt whispered her name and felt her cool hand upon his brow and then his cheek. He attempted to rouse himself, but the brandy and the weariness of the day made it impossible to move even his arms. She was near him, somehow, watching over him and their daughter. She kissed his forehead and Hoyt opened his eyes to smile at her. He felt peace and then surprise when he saw that she wasn't there at all. She had been there—he could still smell the roses—but now Christine had gone.

Yes, now she was gone.

Chapter One

I hadn't had a dream in six months, but I couldn't worry about that right now. Seventy-five of Mobile's most elite and notable women had gathered at the Bragg-Mitchell Mansion to hear me speak about my work at Seven Sisters. I was sure some had come to hear about the crystal chandeliers, the antique ceiling medallions and the expansive Moonlight Garden, but most probably wanted to know how I had "landed" Ashland Stuart. A few others likely wondered if the rumors they had heard about ghosts and such were true. To this crowd of local nobility, I was a nobody, at least in the genealogical sort of way. Even though most Mobilians, the average Jane and Joe, didn't give a hoot about these kinds of things, they really mattered to the old families. For Ashland's sake, I wanted them to accept me on some level.

I had arrived thirty minutes early, and a throng of excited women greeted me at the massive front doors of the mansion. Most were polite, but there were a few unfriendly faces in the crowd. Fortunately, the unspoken rules of polite society did not allow the more curious of my greeters to simply jump in and ask me pointed questions, although it was plain that many of them wanted to.

"You are so lovely! No wonder *our* Ashland was so taken with you," one woman said. She introduced herself, but I instantly forgot her name. I was not too good at remembering the names of the living.

"She certainly is, Margaret! How Sheila cried when she heard Ashland had run off and gotten married!" I wanted desperately to roll my eyes at the idea of Ashland and me "running off" together like naughty teenagers, but I slapped a smile on my face instead. *How do I respond to that?* For the moment, I didn't have to. The ladies remarked on my hair, my pink sheath dress and my fitted green jacket with the three-quarter sleeves.

Is that a Bobbie Brooks dress?

Who does your nails?

Love those shoes! Are they Italian?

I nodded through more introductions and politely smiled as each shared some detail about Ashland with me. Naturally, or so it seemed to the women gathering around me, the conversation steered around to my family name. One lady emerged as the unofficial leader of the group. She was an older woman, my height, with a slim figure and a suspiciously wrinkle-free forehead. She wore pale pink lipstick and expertly applied brown eyeliner that flattered her brown eyes. I couldn't remember her name.

"You from New Orleans, darling? I knew some Jardines from New Orleans once. The family had a delicatessen and muffaletta shop down on Toulouse Street, but it got washed away when the storm came through." The five women surrounding her paused their mini-conversations and observations to listen to my answer. It was unnerving to say the least. *What am I doing here? I almost failed public speaking in college!*

Like a white-haired angel, Bette came to my rescue. "That was Hurricane Katrina," she offered politely. My friend tried to run interference for me, bless her. After all, she had insisted months ago that I come speak about the old house, and I couldn't really refuse her. Bette and I had been through a lot together—we both survived Mia.

"Yes, that's the storm I'm speaking of, Bette." My interrogator continued undeterred, "So you say you're from New Orleans, Miss Jardine—I mean Mrs. Stuart?" She sipped from a white china teacup with a gold band around the rim and an elegantly scripted "B."

"No, I didn't say that. I may have family there, but my mother is from the East Coast."

"Your mother? What about your father? Isn't he a Jardine? Or is that your mother's name?" The older redhead with the perfect afternoon chignon raised her eyebrow as if she had discovered something shocking. I knew my mistake immediately. I wasn't supposed to admit that I didn't know my father or have his last name. *I knew I would screw this up.*

Bette's delighted squeal broke the silence. "Oh look, there is Detra Ann! I am sorry to steal Carrie Jo from you, Mrs. Betbeze, but I have to deliver our speaker to Miss Dowd. No doubt y'all will speak again." Without waiting for a dismissal, Bette gently steered me by the elbow toward a busy Detra Ann, who was greeting a few stragglers. Bette whispered to me as we walked across the perfectly polished wooden floor. "Don't you let that old bat bother you. I have seen her drunk as a foreign sailor and doing the bump at the Mystics Mardi Gras ball, and I swunny! If you shook her family tree, there's no telling what would fall out! Did you know she has an albino sister that nobody sees?"

"Thank you for stepping in."

"No problem. She's as mean as a snake! A snake in designer clothing! The only claim to fame that family has is Yolande Betbeze. She was Miss America in 1951 and, by all accounts, quite a beautiful young woman. Holliday Betbeze needs to get over herself—1951 was a long time ago. Though there's quite a story about Yolande."

Bette always made me smile. I had no idea what "doing the bump" meant, but I laughed thinking about Holliday Betbeze drunk at a ball. "It's okay. It's not like I can hide who I am. You'll have to tell me all about Yolande Betbeze sometime."

"Actually, I was hoping to talk to you later." We stopped about ten feet shy of Detra Ann, who still had not spotted me. "A lot has happened since you've been gone." She dropped her voice and looked around the room before continuing. "I think I found something you should see."

"Really? I'm intrigued." I wanted to know what she was talking about, but it was clear that she was not going to divulge the information with so many ears perked up around us.

As Bette squeezed my hand, her clunky costume ring dug into my skin, but I didn't complain. "You have a special gift, Carrie Jo, and you're not afraid to use it. I admire you for that. It must be hard to dream about someone else's life all the time. Anyway, I won't get into what I wanted to talk about now, but maybe you could come by later this week?"

I nodded, but I felt like such a fake. What would Bette think when I told her the truth? *I don't dream anymore.* What could I say to her? *Sorry, I burned up all my "magic" beating the ghosts of Seven Sisters.*

My dreaming dry spell had me questioning everything. What did it mean? Was it natural? Had I really short-circuited my "power" trying to defeat Isla? I had no idea and knew no one who could mentor me. Funny how you don't appreciate something until you don't have it anymore. I spent so many years trying to pretend that I was normal, and now I would give anything to see Calpurnia and Muncie again.

"Carrie Jo! It's so nice to see you. It has been too long! You look lovely and so tanned—looks like married life has treated you well." Detra Ann had colored her hair during my absence, and the change only made her look more attractive. I could never go blonde—I'd had a bad experience with Sun-In when I was in middle school, and I was sure bleaching my hair would only be worse. The leggy blonde had an angular, beautiful face, and she hugged me as if we were old friends.

At one time her mother had hoped that she and Ashland would hit it off, but fortunately for me, it didn't happen. Detra Ann had fallen hard for Terrence Dale, a talented contractor who worked with us at Seven Sisters. Well, until the supernatural activities weirded him out to the point that he quit. Who could blame him? I sure didn't. I liked TD. We had hit it off from day one. I liked Detra Ann too, but as friendly as she was at this moment, she was changeable. I think Detra Ann primarily did what she wanted to do. As far as marketing went, she was a whiz—but as a future BFF? Probably not. Besides, I had trust issues. My longtime bestie had turned out to be a crazed killer. Apparently, I wasn't too good at judging someone's character.

"I'd say so! Good to see you too. How are things going at the house?" I did not regret our decision to give the house to the City of Mobile, but I did miss it. I longed for the coolness of the Blue Room. I missed the fragrance of the magnolia petals in the Moonlight Garden—I even missed the squeaky stairs and doors. I remembered the first time I walked up the staircase, the cool, smooth wood felt familiar under my fingers. How that first view from the top floor of the grounds below astounded me! It had been love at first sight. Then to discover that I had a heritage there, in a roundabout sort of way, well, that was just incredible.

I did miss it. Even after all the sadness, murder and mystery, I missed Seven Sisters.

"Quite well. We've been packed since the doors opened—people love it, Carrie Jo. You and your team did a remarkable job—you really captured the spirit of the house."

I must have turned a few shades of red because she quickly added, "You know what I mean. We are a month away from Halloween, and we're finally having our first ball." She smiled politely, but Detra Ann was well aware that this subject had been a source of contention between the two of us. When we first met, hosting a ball at Seven Sisters seemed somewhat sacrilegious to me. After all, the ghosts of the past were lingering, unwilling to let go of their lives and their agendas. But that was then—perhaps they'd put all their old bones to rest now. I wanted to believe that, but I knew it wasn't true. Something was undone. Something wasn't right. I could feel the supernatural approaching again, like a lone drum beating in the distance. And just as before, it filled me with anxiety.

Masking my thoughts as well as I could, I smiled at the beautiful, blue-eyed blonde.

"You know it wouldn't be right to have our first ball without you and Ashland in attendance. Would you consider coming?"

"I'll talk to Ashland. He's been so busy with the Dauphin Street project I barely see him. I guess the honeymoon is over now." It was intended as a joke, but it sounded harsh and unhappy.

Bette chimed in, "Now, don't you get discouraged. It takes some adjustment being married. I think you'll find he will come around. He'll balance things out soon. Ashland has a strong work ethic."

Detra Ann chuckled. "He's all work, that's for sure. Please let me know if you can come to the ball. I'll save two tickets for you, just in case. Bette has promised to come—and bring a date."

"Wow, Bette. I'm gone for three months and you find Mr. Right." She chuckled but didn't offer any more information about her mystery date. I wondered if it was her "Steve McQueen" she'd been so crazy about before. "I will do that, Detra Ann. I know that Seven Sisters is in good hands if you're there." I meant it. Like Ashland, Detra Ann loved Mobile and the house. I had no worries that those hallowed grounds would be mistreated.

My heart hurt—I wanted to go home.

"We're offering nightly tours all October, did you hear? Rachel is the best guide—you'd be so proud of her." I smiled thinking of Rachel Kowalski be-bopping from room to room, explaining to the tourists how we acquired the mantelpieces and where the Augusta Evans book collection came from. I wondered what else she might tell them. *"Here's where Hollis Matthews was murdered by an insane historian…and over here, we found the body of Louis Beaumont."*

"I am sure I would be. Rachel is very passionate about local history. I am glad she stayed on with you. How is your mother? Recovering okay?"

Detra Ann frowned and gave an exasperated sigh. "Driving her friends and her nurse crazy. You would hardly know she had surgery; she is on her phone and laptop all the time, still working on behalf of the Historical Society. No way she will be out four more weeks. My guess is she will be back in two, tops. I can't say I'll be sad. That means I can move back to my place even sooner."

I had heard rumors that she and TD had been "playing house" as Bette called it. I was not judging her, but I was curious to hear how he was doing. "I am sure TD will be glad to have you back home."

Her beautiful smile disappeared, and she glanced at Bette reproachfully. "I, uh, TD hasn't been well. He took a trip up to Montgomery, but I think he's home now." She glanced at her watch and promptly changed the subject, "Oh, we better get started." Detra Ann walked away and left me standing by the open French doors.

"Bette? Is TD okay? I get the feeling I said something wrong. What just happened?"

"He left her high and dry." She froze and pressed her lips together thoughtfully. "All men get a little crazy now and then, but that I didn't figure. From all accounts, he's not doing too well. I hear he's had some sort of breakdown."

"Breakdown? What kind of breakdown? Like a mental breakdown? Oh no, this is all my fault."

"No, no, no. Don't take that on yourself. We better head to our seats. My table is right at the back if you need anything." She half hugged me, and I obediently walked toward my seat at the front. I wanted to fuss over my hair and clothing but refrained. My heart sank at the thought that TD was hurting. I remembered seeing his face in the garden the night we fought Isla. He'd dug the hole like a furious dog, trying to locate the box. We'd found it, but at what cost?

I sat in the chair, staring at my empty teacup and saucer. Trays of sweets and sandwiches decorated my table, but I didn't sample any. *Focus on the moment, CJ. You can find out more about TD later.*

I scanned the room as Detra Ann called the meeting to order. Thankfully, most of the tables and guests were behind me so I didn't have to stare at all the faces. Instead, I took in the details of the mansion. This shindig was in one of the front rooms. This particular room had lovely high ceilings, cheerful yellow walls and tons of white molding, decorative columns and a shiny white mantelpiece. A carved marble mantelpiece—in the Federal style, I guessed. The event planner had opted for an intimate setting; there were at least a dozen round tables covered with white linen tablecloths and matching wooden chairs. If I hadn't been so heartsick about TD, I would have cherished every minute of this experience. The Bragg-Mitchell Mansion wasn't as fine as Seven Sisters, but it was one of the loveliest antebellum homes I'd seen in Mobile.

"Now, please make welcome this month's speaker, Carrie Jo Stuart." People began to clap, and I clumsily rose from my chair. Why had I worn heels? Had I learned nothing from history? I was a historian, for Pete's sake.

Carrie Jo Stuart. I still wasn't used to hearing my new name, and I could not help but smile at the friendly applause. I thanked Detra Ann and stood behind the podium, clumsily arranging my notes. My throat felt dry as I stared out at the anxious audience. More than anything, I wanted to jump into the details about our most prized acquisitions. The amazing sculpture in the men's parlor—the delicately carved cherub faces on the mahogany mantelpiece that TD placed in Christine's room. But I didn't.

I decided I would start things a little differently.

Might as well give them something to talk about.

Chapter Two

"Ashland! Are you up there?" I scampered up the stairs to the second floor of our two-story Victorian searching for my husband. According to Ashland, purchasing one of the old homes on Anthony Street was nothing less than miraculous. People loved these homes, and I can't say that I blamed them. From the smooth white exterior to the black cast-iron details, it was a lovely place. Naturally we had worked our magic on the inside, replacing the horrible windows with double-paned Victorian reproductions. This house—Our Little Home, we called it—was indeed little, but it had some historical importance. It was once home to an inventor and author, Mills Broughton. Still, it just didn't feel like home yet.

What did I think? That I would spend my days swanning down the staircase of Seven Sisters, greeting callers in the Blue Room?

"In here!" Ashland called from one of the guest rooms. The soft blue carpet runner felt luxurious underfoot. I pushed on the half-open door and found him rummaging through the closet. "How did it go?" he asked without looking up from his task.

"I nailed it—no tripping or stuttering."

He gave me a disbelieving look.

"Okay, I did get tongue-tied once or twice. Honestly, I am fine." He grinned at me and, as always, I felt my heart do somersaults. He continued to rifle through my carefully stacked closet. I paused to add, "I may have shocked them just a little." I suppose I needn't have told them about my life in Savannah, my brief stint in foster care and how much Mobile felt like home.

"What do you mean? I am sure you were great." His distracted attitude hurt me a little.

"I mean, I told them that I didn't come from an old Southern family. I was just Carrie Jo, historian and researcher."

"Nobody cares about that, CJ. Just you. If you give people a chance, they might surprise you." His voice sounded tired, and I could tell he was in one of his quiet, sulky moods. I wasn't the kind of person to push someone into talking, as I hated that myself, but there were many times in our short history when I wished I knew what he was thinking.

He finally pulled a suitcase from the closet, which triggered a landslide of boxes and bins down on top of him. Laughing, I helped him pick up the books that tumbled out of a blue plastic tub. "We've really got to think about getting a bigger place. Or at least put some things in storage."

"Or you could get rid of some of this stuff. I think most of these are full of your old books and papers."

"I don't have all that much, and I need those for my research. Remember I am supposed to be consulting on the Tillman House. These are important for that project. What about you? I had no idea that you were such a pack rat. You have boxes of baseball cards taking up half the closet." I didn't mean to complain— and I wouldn't have if he hadn't said something first.

"Me? At least I confine my items to the closet. The whole dining room table has become your research center." He frowned, tossing the suitcase on the down coverlet of the queen-sized bed.

Wow, that stung just a tad. His junk didn't really bother me, but I sensed he was angry about something— something about me. "Okay…well, I will do my best to finish my office and keep things off the kitchen table. Um, I'm going to change my clothes—maybe get a shower."

"No need to rush," he said with a sigh, his hands on his hips. "I have to go to New Orleans for a couple of days. I should be back on Sunday."

My shoulders stiffened and my chin jutted out. No way on God's green earth was I going to ask him where he was going. Now I didn't really care! "Two days should be enough time for me to get my office in order. Have fun on your trip."

"It's not that kind of trip—it's mostly for work. I've got to see some people. You can tag along if you like."

"No thanks. Tagging along isn't my style, and I have an office to organize." I strolled out of the room, my hands curled into angry fists intended to keep me from crying.

"Wait. I'm sorry, Carrie Jo. Come back." He shoved a tennis racket and a box of miscellaneous items back into the closet and closed the door. "I didn't mean that crack about your stuff."

I nodded and said, "Okay," leaving the room before he saw the tears in my eyes. It wasn't just this incident—it was where we were now. Like two unhappy strangers forced to live away from home. I walked away, closing the bedroom door behind me, just to let him know that I wanted to be alone for a little while. I knew whatever had ticked him off was not my office.

Everything had been fine during our months in Haiti and the Bahamas, and even afterward when we spent some time on the Happy Go Lucky, Ashland's boat. But those three months were gone, and real life piled in on us. I couldn't help but think maybe we just weren't meant to be together. Perhaps we had rushed into things; the supernatural drama of Seven Sisters forced us to move too fast, too soon. I wondered if that could be true—I suspected he did too. We were from two different worlds. His was respectable, full of tradition, and he was from a family of wealth and means. The world I stepped out of had none of those things. Everything I'd ever had, I had to work hard for, harder than my peers did.

Despite my momentary anger, divorce wasn't a consideration—not for me. I loved Ashland, and I would do my best to make it work, but no way did I plan to be a pushover. *Tag along? What was he thinking?*

Let him go to New Orleans—I could use the time to myself anyway. I stepped into my closet and looked for something to wear. I reached for a pair of old jeans and a soft grey V-neck t-shirt, then went to turn on the shower. As I chewed my fingernail nervously, I heard my phone whistle in my purse. I walked to the dresser and dug it out. It was a text from Ashland.

I'm a jerk.

Walking back into the bathroom, I turned on the shower and stared at the phone. I tapped in my response. *What do you want me to say? That you're not?*

That would be nice.

Sorry. I'm all out of nice.

I threw the phone on the bed, stripped off my clothing and stepped into the warm water. It felt good to be mean for a moment. I typically wasn't very good at mean, but I found married life made me better at it. Not that Ashland wasn't wonderful, thoughtful and completely patient, but living with someone was a new thing for me. I barely had roommates in college because I so treasured my privacy.

When he didn't text me back after a minute or two, guilt washed over me. Maybe this was a good time to test out that old adage that making up was much more fun than breaking up. I wondered how he felt about taking an afternoon shower with me. Before I could call out to him and ask him to join me, I heard the front door slam closed. *Oh well, there goes that idea.*

I rubbed my body down with a thick, soft towel and shimmied into my panties and blue jeans. I pulled on the t-shirt and tucked it into my jeans. I wrapped my waist with a luxurious black leather belt and opted for some black sandals. I pulled my damp hair on top of my head so I could focus on putting on makeup without fighting my wayward wet curls. I laughed when I saw myself in the mirror. I looked, as they sometimes say in Mobile, like a "hot mess." Nothing like Calpurnia and her carefully coiled braids. How times had changed!

"I miss you Calpurnia. Muncie—Janjak, I miss you so much! I hope you're happy where you are," I said to the air around me. I didn't expect to hear anything, and I didn't, but I sensed they were with me still. That both comforted and troubled me. Why weren't they at rest now? For the second time that day, I felt that nagging feeling, like I'd left the water running or the oven on. Something missing, something forgotten—something disturbing.

Putting down the mascara wand for a moment, I closed my eyes. *What is wrong?* I listened to my heart, hoping it would give me a clue, but I heard nothing but the birds chirping outside my spacious bathroom window.

Talking to the air around me I said, "You know, if you're unhappy, all you have to do is tell me. But please—no scary stuff." My phone rang loudly beside me, and I jumped up and out of my vanity chair. "Oh my gosh! You guys have a sense of humor, don't you?" I stared at the phone and picked it up. When I read the screen, my jaw nearly hit the floor. The call was from Terrence Dale!

"Hi, this is Carrie Jo."

"Can you hear me?"

"Yes, I can hear you. How are you, TD?"

"Fine. I need to talk to you—face to face. Can I come by and see you? Or maybe you could come to my place tomorrow? Around four? I should be home by then."

"Sure, I can do that. I'll come to you. Are you still over off Clairborne Street?" I smiled into the phone. I was happy to hear from him.

"Yes, on the corner. I think you've been here once before to pick up something."

"That's right. I'll be there. Would you like me to bring Ashland too?" Reuniting the friends would be a dream come true.

"If it's okay, I'd like it to be the two of us." He didn't offer much explanation, but I chalked it up to male pride. Southern male pride at that. Whatever he wanted to talk about, he didn't want Ashland to know about it.

"I'll see you at four tomorrow."

"Sounds great. Thanks for taking my call."

"Happy to hear from you."

TD hung up the phone, and I walked to the big window that overlooked the backyard. The garden was in a sorry state. The gardenia was overgrown and wilting in the heat, and riotous weeds overran the walkway stones. I couldn't help but think about the Moonlight Garden and how proud TD had been when he finished that project. It had been a thing of beauty— until the three of us tore it up digging for lost treasure.

I held the phone in my hand and pulled up Ashland's name from my contact list but then changed my mind. Why should I tell him about the phone call? He wasn't in an all-fired hurry to tell me who he would see this weekend. Besides, this was just two friends meeting to talk. What was the harm in that?

I felt guilty, even though I had done nothing wrong. Did I really want to start keeping secrets from the man I loved? I walked down the stairs, shocked to see that the front door stood wide open. Crunchy fall leaves had blown in and were strewn down the hall. Piles of them were heaped on the hallway floor as if someone had raked them into a tidy piles. I didn't remember it being so breezy out.

"Ashland?" I stepped out on the porch, past the cheery pumpkins and potted mums. It was only two o'clock, but it was getting cloudy and dark. I could smell the rain on the wind. Looking up and down the sidewalk, I didn't see a soul. Ashland's truck was gone. I walked back inside and called again. Nobody answered. I locked the door and pulled on the knob. I'd have to deal with these leaves but right now, I just wanted to think. I pushed on the door again—now it was closed tight, without even a draft of air around it. I flipped on a light and leaned my back against the door. I coached myself, "Alright, don't be a baby. He probably didn't close the door properly. There's no one here."

Just to be sure I wasn't lying to myself, I walked through the house. Like a teenage girl, I opened every closet just to make sure I was alone. When I had satisfied my overactive imagination, I turned on the radio to a local jazz station. It was too early for wine, but I did help myself to a glass of the peach iced tea Doreen had made us earlier. I had never had a housekeeper before, and the idea had made me uncomfortable at first. But Ashland assured me that he paid Doreen and the rest of his staff well.

Hmm…maybe Doreen had popped in while I was in the shower. Yeah, that was probably it. Anyway, no harm, no foul.

I pretended I didn't hear the faint sound of giggling.

Chapter Three

By six o'clock, I had made a significant dent in the chaos. The built-in bookcases in my office, gifts from Ashland, were full of my research books and a decent collection of leather-bound classics. I arranged them by color first, then changed my mind and lined them up by author. When I was finally satisfied with my library, I turned my attention to the various papers, pictures and other materials I had collected over the years. Ashland had also surprised me with a custom-made desk, deep enough to allow me to spread out my papers but not so long that it hindered access to the French doors leading to the private backyard garden that would one day spring to life. I did love this room; it reminded me of a study in an old 1940s movie, like *Rebecca*, down to the small fireplace on the outside wall. I imagined spending long days here, happily buried in forgotten manuscripts. I wanted to continue working simply because I loved it. That was one reason why I volunteered to help Roz Tillman organize her family's estate. What else would I do with my time if I wasn't working?

One day, Ashland and I would raise a family—I believed that—but now wasn't the time.

Sipping my iced tea, I walked to the window and pulled back the white linen curtain. The sun was sliding down the sky. It would have been the perfect sunset to watch on the Happy Go Lucky. I had meant to catch the sunset earlier, but time had gotten away from me. The jazz station played something by Etta James, which made me miss Ashland all the more. I had stopped checking my phone half an hour ago. He would probably be in New Orleans by now. Maybe I should have tagged along after all.

I opened the door and breathed in the fresh air. The gas lamp kicked on, its amber light casting a few fall shadows in the baleful garden. The all-too-brief rainstorm earlier had blown through, taking with it all the warmth of the day. I closed my eyes and enjoyed the coolness. I toyed with the idea of abandoning my office project and maybe grabbing a bite to eat somewhere—I'd made so much progress already—but then my neighbor stepped out on his porch. I couldn't see him, but I could hear his very private phone conversation. Closing the door as discreetly as I could, I stepped back inside. I turned the lock and nearly jumped out of my skin for the second time.

Someone walked past my door quickly and without saying a word to me.

"Doreen? Is that you?" Setting the glass down on the corner of the desk, I walked into the hallway. "Doreen?" I froze—the front door was standing wide open once again. More leaves were in the hallway, as if someone had deliberately brought in baskets of shriveled leaves and scattered them on the hardwood floor. My half hour of work sweeping them all out earlier had been for naught. I turned off the radio and called again, "Doreen? Ashland?" Chills ran down my spine. *I know I saw someone!* I walked to the front door and closed it again. *And I know I locked this door!*

I didn't bother calling again. Something was happening, but the ghosts of the past were silent, at least the ones I knew personally. The urge to flee was overwhelming. I ran back to the dining room and grabbed my keys and purse off the sideboard. Just as I turned to walk out, I noticed a fat, worn envelope resting on top of a stack of unopened envelopes. As frightened as I felt, it caught my attention. I didn't remember ever seeing it, and I had been working in this room and the adjoining one all afternoon. It was addressed to me with no return address, but that didn't matter. I recognized the tight, controlled handwriting.

This was from Mia! Had she been here? Had she escaped from the facility?

I stared at the return postmark. It had arrived a month ago—no wonder I hadn't seen it. Ashland and I had been gone for months. Why would Doreen set this here and not where she put the rest of the mail? That familiar, unsettled feeling began to creep over me. No, I didn't want to be here anymore. Not right now. Taking the envelope with me, I left my Victorian home behind. I pulled onto Government Street and headed to Bette's house. Anywhere would be better than here, and I could use some comfort and advice. As I closed the door behind me, I heard a stifled giggle. It was her— Isla was here! In my house!

Stopping at the red light just past my house, I reminded myself to breathe. My knuckles were white—I had a death grip on the steering wheel. This was no time to freak out. Surely I was wrong. We had defeated Isla, right? Breaking my rule about using my phone while driving, I dug in my purse. I had to talk to Ashland, now! Trying to beat the light change, I tapped on the screen and called my husband. "Hi, this is Ashland…" Voicemail. Rats! How would that message sound?

"Honey, please come home. I think the ghost is back." I tossed the phone back in my purse.

Focus on the road, girl! It was a pleasant drive for a Friday night. Not a ton of cars out on the normally busy street, and many of the old houses along Government were decorated for fall. The sight of porches full of pumpkins and the trees draped with goofy sheets meant to look like ghosts helped calm my nerves. Still a bit panicked, I pulled into Bette's driveway. From the road I could see that she wasn't home, and my heart sank in my chest. Her light blue convertible, a gift from Ashland and me, was gone and the house lights except the side porch light were off. I pulled into the driveway just to have a place to think for a minute. I checked my phone again but Ashland hadn't bothered to call me back. *What was going on with him?*

Glancing up at my old apartment, I wished I could barge in and make myself at home. That's where my life here in Mobile had begun, in Bette's over-the-garage apartment. I missed that place. Bienville, Bette's orange tabby, was nowhere to be found. I spied Iberville, his less than friendly brother, staring at me from the gardenias that grew beneath Bette's kitchen window. Now what? My appetite had disappeared, but I didn't want to go back to the house right now. I tore open the package on the seat next to me. All that was inside was a scrap of paper and a worn leather-bound book. With some trepidation, I unfolded the note. Yes, this was from Mia.

Nothing I can say will ever make up for what I have done. However, after reading this, maybe you will understand.
–M

Refolding the note, I examined the unusual book cover. The leather cover was embossed with the image of a peacock showing his feathers. Flipping on the map light, I studied it closer: *The Stars that Fell* by E. Halderon. I didn't see anything that jumped out at me as I leafed through the pages, just faded letters on delicate paper. I closed the book and slid it back in the envelope. Now wasn't the time to read an old book from a former friend. Lightning cracked across the sky in the distance. I had to go somewhere—I couldn't just hang out in Bette's driveway all night.

Seven Sisters! Detra Ann mentioned that they were having nightly tours during October. I put the car in reverse and made the quick trip to the plantation. It had been three months since I had stepped foot on the property, and the thought of returning thrilled me. Maybe my former intern and fellow historian Rachel Kowalski would be there. I turned down the long drive that led to the house. Someone had trimmed back the hedges, and I could see the top floor of Seven Sisters shining brightly all the way down the driveway.

It was barely dark, but there were half a dozen cars in the driveway, presumably to take the Halloween tour. I was thankful there were no inflatable cartoon witches on the lawn or plastic bats hanging from the live oaks. Detra Ann and her crew had lined the pathway to the house with hurricane glasses that held white flameless candles. It was lovely and simple, evoking a certain understated magic.

I parked the car, stuffed Mia's envelope in my purse and followed the sidewalk to the massive front steps. I paused at the bottom, remembering the first moment I stood here, the night I met Ashland. He had emerged from the overgrown brush like a phantom, but his easy smile had won my heart.

Standing near the front door was a perky young woman, an Azalea Trail Maid, according to her massive purple antebellum dress. The gown moved as she waved to me and walked to the porch edge. She handed me a tour brochure. "Hi! The next tour starts in 30 minutes, but you can step into the foyer and enjoy some refreshments."

"No, thank you. I am not here for the tour. Is Rachel around? Rachel Kowalski?"

"Um, I'm not sure. I don't really work here, but the lady in charge, Miss Dowd, is inside. Maybe she can help you."

"Alright, thank you." I smiled at the teenager and walked through the open door. How different it was now than the first moment I saw it! No more lumpy carpet and musty rooms. The walls were meticulously painted, and hardwood floors shone brilliantly throughout the house. Someone had placed a round table in the foyer, covered with more brochures and information about local historical landmarks. I didn't like that, but the house wasn't mine anymore. Not that it ever really was. It had belonged to Ashland's family, but now it was just another historical property owned by the City of Mobile. Nobody greeted me in the lobby, so I made myself at home. I walked first to the ladies' parlor, where everything was exactly where I left it. As I looked around the room, scenes from my dreams played out in my head. Over by the fireplace was where

Calpurnia had first laid eyes on David Garrett. It was such a sad room, really. The side door was closed, but I could hear voices in the Rose Garden.

"I'm sorry, ma'am, but the tour is in the Moonlight Garden now. Just out the back door. Oh, Carrie Jo! I didn't know you were here." It was Detra Ann, surprised but polite.

Suddenly, I didn't know what to say. "I was just in the neighborhood. I mean, I thought I could…"

"No need to explain. Come on into the Blue Room. We can chat in there unless you prefer to sit in here."

"No, the Blue Room is fine." I followed behind her, anxious to see what my old office looked like now. The walls were still painted a cool blue. Calpurnia's painting hung over the fireplace, as it should. All of our desks and equipment had been removed, replaced with period furniture. There was a modern piece, a small love seat, by one of the tall windows. Detra Ann and I sat, and I fumbled for what to say. I needn't have worried; she was still the take-charge kind of gal. *Like I used to be before all this. What happened to me?*

"What can I help you with, Carrie Jo?"

"I, uh, I just wanted to come by and see the place. It feels like forever since I walked these halls."

Detra Ann sat with perfect posture on the couch beside me. I felt an awkward smile stretch across my face. She gave me a sweet smile of her own in return. "I understand that. This place must feel like home. You are always welcome to stop by, Carrie Jo. You know, you're kind of a legend around here. Chip and Rachel just adore you."

"That's sweet to say. Those two were hard workers, and I am glad that at least Rachel is still here. I guess Chip got the job at the Mobile Museum?"

"No, he didn't. To his credit, there was some stiff competition. He has been lurking around here, mostly to see Rachel, I think. He spends a lot of time working with his professor in the northern part of the county. Some project trying to find the old fort, Fort Louis de La Louisiane."

"That's interesting. Wow, if they found the actual location—that would be such an important find." She nodded and then we sat quietly again, the sound of the clock ticking on the fireplace filling the emptiness between us. Seven Sisters still had the comforting smell of wet paint and fresh wood. Maybe we had done something good after all, Ashland and I.

Detra Ann's blue eyes scrutinized me. "I know why you're really here, Carrie Jo."

I caught my breath. "You do?" *You know that I'm hearing and seeing things again? That I'm not dreaming and that my husband barely talks to me anymore?*

"Yes, you're here about TD. Aren't you?"

I didn't know what to say. *I came here because I think Isla Beaumont is in my house.* "I won't deny that I am curious. What's actually going on, Detra Ann? Bette mentioned he had some sort of breakdown?"

She leaned back against the love seat, her posture collapsing under the obvious weight of their relationship. She slipped off her heels and sighed. "You could call it that. All I know is that things were going along fine, and then the incident in the Moonlight Garden happened. Everything went downhill after that. He tried to get over it—I tried to help him—but it didn't happen. He had nightmares, bad nightmares. He'd wake up screaming."

I hadn't known that. How would I have? "Did you ever get him to go to church? You mentioned giving that a try."

She nodded. "He went, but I guess he never found the answers he was looking for. Honestly, I don't know how to help him. I am crazy about him—as you well know—but I am not going to date a man who refuses to work and mopes around all day. Have you seen him lately?"

Now was the time for some honesty. I couldn't keep it from her. "He called me earlier. Says he wants to talk. I am supposed to meet him tomorrow afternoon."

"Carrie Jo, I know you have a big heart, and I care about TD too. But he's not the same guy you remember. He is angry all the time. The littlest things set him off. I mean, I do not think he would harm you, but then again, he is not the laid-back, sweet person we used to know. He is moody and…" Her pretty freckled nose crinkled. "He drinks a lot. One of my brothers is an alcoholic. I know the signs, and I refuse to enable TD."

"I owe this to him. I feel responsible for what happened. If it were not for me, for my dreaming, we would have never been in that garden digging around. I am the reason he is drinking. I have to make it right."

Detra Ann reached across the love seat and took my hand. "You can't help who you are, any more than I can or anyone else can. You did not make TD drink. He fell apart on his own." I nodded, but I was not convinced. "Look at all the good that has happened, Carrie Jo. Now we know what happened here. Calpurnia can rest now. All of them, they can rest because we all know the truth. That's no small thing."

"No, it's not," I agreed. *But they're not all resting!*

Chapter Four

"Detra Ann, I have a huge favor to ask you. You do not have to say yes, but I need to ask it anyway."

"Okay, what is it?" She looked at me intently, waiting for me to spill the beans. Would she think I was crazy? Until this conversation, I would never have believed that Detra Ann cared about how I felt, not one bit.

"First, I promise you, I will help TD. Whatever has passed between you two, I know you belong together, just like Ashland and I do. I can't explain it, but I know." She gave a tiny smile. "Fight for what you have—what you want, Detra Ann. Pray for it. Be patient...he's going to come back around. Whatever is bothering him, we'll uncover it, but I need you to help me."

"What do you mean? I don't understand."

How to explain when I wasn't sure myself? "TD had a part in what we uncovered. He helped us—he's probably experiencing the same kind of resistance we have."

Her big blue eyes widened. "You mean like spiritual resistance?"

"That would be my guess. Now you see why I have to help him—I know Ashland would want that too. Honestly, ever since that night, nothing has been the same. Not for me, not for Ashland. Obviously not for TD."

Detra Ann's eyes betrayed her feelings. She was telling the truth: she didn't understand, and she was definitely afraid.

"You have to keep fighting. There's nothing anyone, dead or alive, can do to keep you apart—not if you were meant to be together!"

At that moment, a glass figurine from a nearby side table, one of the less expensive ones in the arrangement, flew off the mantelpiece and shattered on the floor at our feet. Both of us jumped up, careful to avoid the glass.

Detra Ann clutched my hands, and we just stood there and waited for more strange activity, but nothing happened. Detra Ann breathed a sigh of relief. "What just happened?"

"I'm not really sure, but someone or something did not like our conversation. That means we're going the right way! That's where I need your help."

"Anything. What is it?" Still looking around the room nervously, Detra Ann slipped her heels back on.

"I want to spend the night here, in Calpurnia's room—no, wait. In Christine's room. I won't harm anything, and I can't really explain it, but I feel compelled to stay. You see, I know I missed something. A piece of the puzzle is missing. When I find it, all will be well."

"You want to dream, don't you? I don't know. What would Ashland say about this, Carrie Jo? He loves you so much. If you were hurt, or if something happened to you, he would never forgive me."

"Nothing is going to happen. I am going to sleep with the lights on, but I need to try and dream here. I can't help but feel that I left something undone. I missed something. We missed something. I have to find out what and make it right. Worst of all, Isla is still wandering around. Although I haven't seen her yet, not fully, I know it's her. I need her to be gone! Please, let me stay just this one time."

Detra Ann smiled. "Okay, on one condition—no, two conditions. First, I stay with you, and second, you come to the Halloween Ball here. Agreed?"

"That's not necessary. I can stay alone. I swear I'm not afraid to be alone."

"I am sure you aren't, but you won't be. That's the deal, take it or leave it." She wasn't budging, and strangely enough, I was glad. I hated the idea of taking part in a ball. I was the worst dancer on the planet! But if it meant I could stay at Seven Sisters, I would just have to put on my dancing shoes and a smile.

"Fine, agreed, but we can't sleep together." Her look of surprise spoke volumes. I chuckled. "No! I mean in the same bed. You see, when I dream, there is a chance I can transfer and see your dreams too. I don't want to know what you are thinking when you are dreaming. That's an invasion of your privacy. You can stay in the other room or set up a cot in Christine's room. But are you sure you want to do this?"

"Yes! I want to see a real dream catcher in action! This is all new to me!"

"Well, I'll go call Ashland. I hate to go back to the house tonight. It's getting late."

"No worries, I'll call my housekeeper. She can bring us both some clothes and toothbrushes and toothpaste, whatever we need." We made a little list, including some food, and waited until the guests left. At about 10 p.m., we walked up the stairs to go to bed. My call with Ashland didn't happen. I did get a hold of him once, but the music in the background was so loud that I couldn't hear him. Angry, I hung up and put my phone on mute. I didn't want to hear it if he called me back. I had to focus now. I had to rein in my emotions and focus on Christine.

Maybe that's what I'd missed! What happened to her? To her baby? That had to be it!

I opened the door to Christine's room. I loved this room—it never got a ton of sunshine during the day, but it was bright and had a serene view, even in Christine's day. After I changed into the pinstriped capri pajamas that Detra Ann brought me and we chitchatted a while, we lay down to sleep. I took the bed, which wasn't the original but was in the right spot in the room. We'd brought in a rollaway bed for Detra Ann. She moved it to the corner of the room and made it up neatly with pink sheets.

She piled her blond hair on top of her head in a ponytail and looked at me expectantly. She didn't look a bit tired. "I'm nervous as heck. What do I do?"

I smiled at her. "You don't have to do a thing. I might read a little before I go to sleep. Sometimes it helps me relax."

"Listen, do you really think this will help TD? You weren't just putting me on?"

"I would never joke about this kind of thing, but it's just a hunch. You see, we all had a connection. Ashland was connected to Calpurnia, I was connected to Muncie, but TD...I'm not sure about."

"I see."

"I sound like a crazy person, but all I can tell you is what I think and feel. There are no books I can read that teach me about all this stuff. You know, growing up, I never considered myself a spiritual person. But I guess I am. Weird how that works."

"No, I get it. I've never seen anything. Except that fan stopping on the porch and the figurine crashing earlier. And both of those things happened with you around."

I hadn't thought about that before. She had a point.

"Another thing. If everyone involved is connected, who was Mia connected to?"

"That's what we need to figure out—and what happened to Christine. That's important, that much I know."

We chatted some more until Detra Ann began to yawn. "If you don't mind, I'm going to plug in my headphones and listen to some music. It's kind of my nighttime routine. I love sleeping to music. It drives TD crazy, but it helps me sleep."

"Sure, go ahead. Is this light going to bother you?"

"Not at all. I don't have a problem sleeping with the lights on. In fact, it might help because I admit I'm a little freaked out. Not because of you—because of what happened earlier."

"I get that. Me too, but I don't feel any sort of presence right now. Thanks, by the way. I appreciate you allowing me to do this."

She was quiet for a minute. "I have never known anyone like you, Carrie Jo. Before I met you, I thought that supernatural stuff was nothing but hokum—just shills trying to make money on whoever would believe them. But you're not like that. You're just a real person. Have you always dreamed about ghosts?"

I had never thought of it like that, and I admitted it to her. "I always just thought of it as dreaming. When I was a kid, I thought everyone did it, but I learned the hard way that I was wrong. Completely."

"What did your parents think? Are they supportive about your…powers?"

"I would hardly call it a power," I said with a laugh, "but I can see why someone would think that. Until I came to Seven Sisters I considered it more of an impediment. It used to drive my mother crazy. I don't think she knew what to do with me. She never quite got it. She thought I could turn it off, like I was having these dreams on purpose. It upset her to think I could see people's dreams."

"So she wasn't a dreamer? A dream catcher?"

"If she was, she never told me."

"What about your dad? Did he dream?"

"I don't know. I never met him."

"Oh, I'm sorry."

"It's okay. You can't miss what you've never known, right?"

"I guess that's true. Well, Ashland sure loves you." She stretched out on the rollaway and smiled. "I've known him all my life and have never seen him fall in love before—ever. Don't get me wrong, there have been plenty of girls interested in him, but he's always been kind of standoffish. Never committing to anyone. I am so glad he has you."

I was curious to hear about my husband from someone who knew him better than I did. "Bette told me that your mother used to hope the two of you would get together."

She chuckled. "My mother is a control freak. Ashland and I kind of got one another—we left each other alone. He was always talking about what he'd like to do for Mobile, how he wanted to restore his family's name. I was always talking about leaving this city. Little did I know I would end up loving it too." She chewed her lip and added, "Everyone in Ashland's world wanted something from him. Hollis wasn't the only one who wanted his money. I felt sorry for him—he got used a lot. Our senior year, we used to skip school together and go to the beach, but I swear nothing ever happened. We didn't like each other that way."

I smiled. "I'm glad he had a friend."

"What else did Bette tell you about me?"

"Nothing bad. Well, except that you were cross-eyed. Imagine my surprise when I met you and you were just drop-dead gorgeous."

"Ha! Don't I wish!" She laughed aloud. "I had a lazy eye for like one summer, but the eye doctor corrected it with a patch. What an amazing summer that was—me wearing a patch for three months, all the guys running the other way. It did do one thing, though. It made me more sympathetic toward people with physical challenges."

"Yes, I guess it would."

She yawned and smiled. "I guess I'm going to try and sleep. If you need me, I'm right here. Kick that fan up a notch, will you?"

"Sure." I slid out of bed and turned up the oscillating fan. It was comfortable to me, but then again this old house didn't have central air and heating. Before I got back into bed, I dug the envelope out of my purse.

Detra Ann had her back to me; she was playing on her phone listening to music. I examined the envelope again and sighed. Why was I doing this? Could I trust anything that Mia might tell me? What did I care about her reasons for trying to kill me—and William? She did kill Hollis Matthews and God knows who else.

Nothing else to see, just my name and new address and a crumpled envelope. I pulled out the book inside and held it under the yellow lamp light. It was apparently the first in a collection of biographies of actors and actresses. The words *THE STARS THAT FELL* were embossed with gold, or they had been. I could see a just fleck or two of gold now. I ran my fingers over the peacock and opened the cover.

Published in 1921 by the Nelson-Howell Publishing Company. Well, so what? What did this have to do with Mia? Another delusion?

I leaned back against the pillows and closed my eyes for a minute. Mia was crazy—there was no doubt about that—but she had been right about so many things. When it came to research and hunches, she was the best. I felt a twinge of sadness. Mia had been the first to discover that the Beaumont treasure was real and the first to have an idea of where it might be. She was right about the fact that the statues were a map, a map that was echoed with the markers in the Cottonwood cemetery. She knew, even before I did, that Calpurnia had never found the treasure.

I held the book to my chest and took a deep breath. I guess it was time to know what else Mia knew. I hoped I wouldn't regret this.

I probably would.

Chapter Five

I could tell the book was old by the font and the page layout. And I recognized that "old book" scent, probably one of my favorite smells in the world. The book began with a note from the author and some commentary about his subjects, which included a woman named Delilah Iverson.

Dear Reader,

I am not merely an author but a collector of unusual lives. THE STARS THAT FELL is a representation of my life's work. Many of you, no doubt, will recognize some of the more famous names like Delilah Iverson, Nate Daniels and Edwin McCarthy.

I must confess that it took some convincing on my part to compel my first subject, the talented Miss Iverson, to agree to speak to us concerning personal matters. In the end, she graciously yielded to my pleas and allowed me that privilege. As I have such great respect for the lady and consider her a dear friend, her story begins THE STARS THAT FELL.

Your Faithful Scribe,

Ernesto Halderon

I flipped to the first chapter and read the first few sentences. Nothing unusual yet. I sighed and hunkered down in my bed, reading by the dim light. A light pattering of rain began tapping against the window. The house was quiet except for the occasional squeak of wood, which one would expect in a house as old as this.

Dear Ernesto,

What should I say? So, you wish to hear my story? I am willing to tell it, but I insist on doing the telling. Perhaps if you knew how crowded my mind would become with the faces of those who are gone, those I have loved and lost, you would forget this idea, have mercy and find a more worthy muse for your book. Yet I can see by the anxious look on your face that you will not allow me to depart without first having told all.

For myself, I cannot imagine that any intelligent person would care to read about my life, for I have not found it so unusual or interesting. Surprising? Yes! But it was my life, and I have enjoyed every sun-filled and rainy day included within it. Even when the storms came and the war rolled over the South like the devil drove it, I wanted to live! I guess you could say that I have a strong will to live. As I am now seventy, this I certainly have proven.

Where shall I start? Should I tell you all my secrets? Whom I have loved and whom I have hated? Should I tell you about the stolen kisses, the promises we made and the inevitable betrayals? Should I tell you about the time I missed my happiness by mere minutes? Oh, but those were the times when I felt the most alive, alive in my pain! If it's a tale you want, then a tale you shall get.

Hmm… I liked her already.

***

My life began quite happily, dear Ernesto. I was not born with a silver spoon in my mouth—quite the contrary! At an early age, I learned the value of hard work, and it is not a lesson I regret having learned. Yet we had fine things when it was possible. Hard work has paid me well, as you can see by my many achievements here. But things were different then.

My parents, Jacob and Katharine Iverson, owned a sundries shop in downtown Mobile, Alabama. My father was also a master carpenter, and his fine Norwegian workmanship was always in high demand. Our shop was right on Conception Street, across from the Irish church that rang bells for matins and whenever a good Catholic child was born in the parish that surrounded it. Near our shop was the dress and hat shop where I later went to work. Our home was above the sundries shop. It was nothing large, but I had my own room, which was quite a treat for the time.

My brother and I spent many happy days there until right before the war. My parents loved America, but my father had no desire to take sides in a war that would divide the great country he so passionately loved. My parents weren't quite Southerners yet, although they loved living in Mobile. My mother always said that Norway was the most beautiful place on Earth but Alabama was certainly the warmest. She liked that. She told me on many occasions that the cold hurt her bones.

My brother had other ideas. Neither he nor I remembered Norway, although he was born there. I was four years younger than Adam, and we were very close, as close as a brother and sister could be. I was born an American, born at home in Mobile. Although he had been born in Norway, Adam was a Southerner through and through. I still remember him young and happy. He had the blondest hair; it always fell in his eyes. Mother would say, "Delilah, cut your brother's hair. He looks like a sheepdog." We would take the chair out behind the shop, and I would cut his hair as best I could. He was kind to me, even when I cut gaps into his hair or made him look like a beggar boy. He would say, "Yes, this is what I wanted, thank you, Delilah." I would smile, and he would give me a coin, just like I had been a true barber. He always had a way of making me feel special.

When other young men his age began to sign up to serve in the Confederate Army, he felt it his duty to do the same. Mind you, we were not slave owners; my parents abhorred slavery, but they equally abhorred the heavy taxation by the Northern states—it was a concern for all local businessmen and indeed businessmen everywhere I would imagine. For many men, that alone was enough reason to go to war. They were fighting for their wealth and happiness. There were plenty of raw materials in the South but no way to manufacture anything. All those factories were up North. Mobile was the Cotton Queen, but she had nary a one cotton processing company.

What arguments my father and Adam would have on this subject! That was a difficult time for all of us. I was only fifteen when the talks of war turned serious; Adam was nineteen and a young man—ready to prove himself as such. My Uncle Lars wrote us inviting us to travel to Canada until the war was over. That idea didn't sit well with my brother; he knew that the local families would call our father and him a yellow coward.

"It's always better to fight," Adam would say to Poppa. Then Poppa would speak Norwegian, and Adam would join him. I couldn't understand a word they were saying. I always regretted that. Eventually, it would become clear that Adam had lost the argument. At the request of Uncle Lars, we prepared to head north to Canada to ride out the war. I didn't want to leave my hometown, but I also didn't want to see the city destroyed. It surely would be—and to some degree it was! Adam was angry, of course. As a grown man, he could make his own decision. I knew he wanted to leave us. I couldn't let him go!

I had followed Adam that afternoon. I watched him walk into the military station and talk to the sergeant. He had not yet signed up, but I knew he was intending to do so. That evening, when Poppa put the violin away and Mother finished the dinner dishes, I ran upstairs and went into Adam's room. He was in bed, wearing his nightgown, his hands behind his head. He stared out the far window, looking at the moon.

"What is it, Lila?"

I sulked toward him and crawled in the bed with him. "You cannot leave me, Adam. You would send me all the way to a land where I know no one. All the way to Canada."

"Hush now. You want me to be a kid forever. It's only for a little while, and then I will be home with my jacket full of metals and ribbons."

"That's not what will happen, and you know it." I held him tight as if it could really be the last time I saw him. He held me too.

"I don't know anything of the sort." He rubbed my hair playfully. "Wouldn't you feel proud to have a brother who served in the war? Wouldn't you want me to show them that I am not a coward?"

"Yes, you could show them, but then I would lose you. That's not fair, Adam. You would do this just to show off?" I sat up, my dark curls falling around my face.

Adam took my hand and kissed it. "You'd better go to bed, Lila. Tomorrow's going to be a big day."

I walked slowly to the wooden door, my lower lip quivering. "Please don't do this, Adam. Will you make me a promise?"

He rolled back over to face me. "What is it?"

"If it is raining in the morning, you will stay with us. If it's sunny, you will go. Isn't that fair?"

"Really? That's the deal you want me to make?" He smiled sadly and covered back up. I was an excellent deal maker—just ask anyone who came to the shop. "That's too easy. You know it's going to rain tomorrow."

"Okay then, let's say that if you see a rainbow in the morning sometime before 8 a.m., you will stay." Even as I said the words, I could see Adam actually seeing the rainbow and then looking at the clock. My mother called it intuition; I mostly kept my knowings and seeings to myself, but that day was special.

Adam laughed at the idea. "Not giving yourself much of a chance to win, Lila. You do like these silly tests, don't you? Okay, I agree. If I see a rainbow tomorrow before 8 a.m., I will stay with you and our parents. We will go to Canada. If not, I go to join the Army. That is a deal. Now go to bed."

"Thank you, Adam!" I slipped out of his room feeling as if I had won the argument. Somehow I knew that God was on my side. Adam would see a rainbow, and he would be okay. Best of all, we would be together.

Little did I know he would hate me for it later.

Chapter Six

Closing the book quietly, I placed it on the nightstand. I didn't want to sleep with it. She wasn't the girl I wanted to see right now. Her story was beginning to intrigue me, especially in light of the fact that THE STARS THAT FELL was on Mia's required reading list.

The truth was I wanted to see Christine, to dream about her. Strangely enough, I felt complete peace. I knew I was doing the right thing. I felt no fear that I would see snakes or be chased by horrible monsters. I simply whispered "Christine Beaumont Cottonwood…" quietly until I slipped into my dream.

The air around me moved fast at first, and then suddenly it stopped. I was in Miss Christine's room, standing at the end of the bed. I was standing behind the doctor who was sweating so hard he asked me to wipe his brow with my apron. I did as I was told. My name was Hannah, and I was new to Seven Sisters. I came from some place called Philadelphia, a long way from here. My former mistress, a woman who ran a house of ill repute in the Blue District, lost me in a card game to one of her rich lovers. It had been a joke to her, sending me away from the only family I had ever known. How she laughed and drank and laughed some more that night. Fortunately, my new master was a nice man who taught piano. He moved to Mobile, but he died quite suddenly from pains in his chest.

I come upstairs to bring him his morning cornbread and milk mush, and the old man was cold dead. I didn't know what to do, so I sat down, ate the mush and then walked down to the sheriff's office to tell him the news. Soon, I was sold to another family, and some folks say I was very lucky to get to work at Seven Sisters. It was a grand place with many rooms and plenty of food to eat. But it was full of sadness. Everyone here was sad. At least at Madame LaMont's everyone was happy, but that was probably because they were always drunk. Here, in this big fine house, it was like they was all under some sort of magical spell, the kind that slowly crept in and couldn't be removed no matter how many prayers you say.

The baby's head began to show, but Miss Christine never made a sound. She tried to sit up a few times but refused to speak. She just stared up at the ceiling. Her mouth was slack, and Hooney had to wipe it often. "Miss Christine, please try. Push that baby out, Miss Christine. You'll feel so much better if you do." Hooney pleaded with her kindly, but the woman was gone. She was like the living dead. It broke my heart.

"Hannah, come up here for a minute and let me come help the doctor. You stand right here and wipe her mouth when she needs it. And talk to her kindly. Help her remember who she is and what she is doing. We need her to push that baby out, or the doctor here might have to cut her open."

Hooney's voice was dead serious, and I didn't want that to happen to Miss Christine. She had been a nice lady. She'd given me a new cotton dress and apron when I got here. She'd even made sure that I found a pair of secondhand shoes that fit me well.

"Miss Christine, please wake up." Hannah patted my face with her hand and suddenly….

I wasn't Hannah anymore. How weird was this? My gift was changing, and I didn't understand it at all.

Now I was Christine.

I feel warm, like I have too many clothes on. Oh, to be alone and naked with Hoyt! I would take a thousand beatings for him. How I love that man! When will I see him again? Look! There's our daughter! There's Calpurnia, over there in the corner. Why does she look so sad? Don't cry, Callie. I have something for you. I know you will find it.

I wrote you a note, dearest. "Find your True Self, and you will Find a Treasure." I hope you understand. You are our treasured daughter, our daughter. I wish I could tell you…

Oh…why does my stomach hurt so badly? I scream and scream and scream, but nobody hears me. Whose dark face is that leaning over me? I want Ann-Sheila! Where is my friend? No, she's gone. Like Louis.

Louis! Louie! Come back to me!

Look, there's baby Calpurnia trying to walk in her new shoes. How proud I am! My daughter! How she would hate me if she knew my secret! Oh, the pain is excruciating! Why can't someone see that I am in pain?

My Mother used to say that pain was proof that you were alive. That pain was essential for living. Once we stopped hurting, we stopped living. I want you now, Mother! How you would disapprove of Hoyt and me, but he is a good man! I married the man Father wanted me to marry, and see what it has brought me? Nothing but sadness and ruin. Mother, Mother, please don't go. Take me with you.

I try to sit up and follow her, but she leaves the room, a swirl of blue silk behind her.

I see another face now...Isla! NO! NO! Get her away from me! So much like Olivia but so evil! She is my tormentor. The things she told me! I feel the darkness surrounding me!

The lies! Oh the lies she tells me, Louis! My beautiful brother! It cannot be true!

Hoyt! Hoyt! I hear your voice. Help me, please, my love! My own darling! Help me. Please watch over our children. They need you—I need you. Maybe the day will come when you and I can be together truly. How I long for that day. No more sneaking to the cottage, hoping and praying that no one catches us! I would do it all again, all for love, all for my family!

What lovely roses! Who so kindly brought me roses? May I smell them? Bring them closer.

Again, the dark-faced girl is leaning over me. I barely see her smile as she shows me a baby. Is that Calpurnia? I feel a surge of wetness between my legs, but the pain has gone. What has happened? The room has darkened! It is too dark, and I hear voices that I cannot understand.

No, the voices have stopped. All is quiet. All is quiet. A little rest now...

What is that sound? It is the sound of thunder—it is Jeremiah! Make him leave, Hoyt! You do not know how he beats me. How he hurts me. If only you could hear me. Where am I?

I am coming, Calpurnia. My child is crying. Mother is coming now!

Hannah wiped at Christine's face again.

Wait…Christine saw me! I saw her look at me! She saw me! *Who are you?* her mind asked. Her face did not move.

I am a friend, Christine. I am here to help you.

Are you an angel? Are you here to take me to heaven?

My heart melted in my chest. How could this be happening? She couldn't really see me, could she?

Before I could answer her, I was Hannah again.

"Get that baby out of my sight!"

I winced at the master's anger. He would never hit me with his leather strap, but he had beaten many others at Seven Sisters. He leaned over the bed and yelled at Miss Christine, who could not hear him. I muffled a cry as I watched him.

"You were supposed to get me a son, wife! Not another daughter! A son! You have failed me for the last time! Everyone out!"

The doctor stood to face him, his face wet with sweat or tears or both. "No, sir, I shall not leave my patient, even if you beat me with an inch of my life. Your wife has wounds that will kill her if we leave them like this. I will not allow you to harm her!"

"Damn you too, Page! You nosy bastard! Always here sniffing around, sniffing at the skirts in this house. You do what you have to do, then you get out of here. Or I will call the sheriff to come and drag you out. You forget your place, sir."

"On the contrary, I forget nothing." Dr. Page stood up and tossed a bloody cloth to the ground, his hands clenched in angry fists.

With a grunt of disapproval, the master left us alone, at least for a little while. The doctor finished his ministrations but lingered at Miss Christine's bedside. He held her hand and spoke to her quietly, but the missus never looked his way. I thought maybe I saw a hint of a smile on her face, and then nothing but emptiness. Hooney stood on the other side of the bed, sniffing and wiping tears from her face. She whispered prayers, the kind of prayers the missus often said, and made the sign of the cross.

The doctor gave Hooney instructions on how often to give the medicine he was leaving. "I shall be back in the morning to see her. These drops will only help with the pain, nothing else. She needs to be in a hospital. I'll see what I can do to make that happen. In the meantime, you keep him away from her."

"I don't know who can stop him if he means to get to her. All we can do is pray."

"Well, don't defy him, but at least send for me. Surely you can do that. I will not stand by while he kills his wife. The lady needs to rest if she's ever to come out of her sickness."

Hooney promised and put the sleeping baby in my arms. I peered down at her face: she was peaceful, unaware that her Daddy was evil and that her Momma had lost her mind. I wondered what kind of life she would have.

A few hours later, the doctor was long gone and the master was deep into a bottle of corn whiskey. He came staggering back up the stairs, yelling for his wife. Instead, he found me in the nursery with his baby daughter. "That baby is dead," he growled, wavering on his feet.

"What? No, sir. She's not dead—she's sleeping like an angel. She is a beautiful little girl." I smiled, but my insides were frightened and my alarm was screaming at me to run.

"I don't think you heard me right, girl. That baby is dead. You hear me? Dead! Now get rid of it. I don't want no dead baby around here stinking up the place."

I stared at him, blinking wildly. What should I do?

Mr. Cottonwood cast an evil grin. "Want me to show you it's dead?" He reeled toward me but I stepped back, avoiding his snatch easily. The baby began to stir and fuss.

"No! Please! I understand, sir! This baby is dead. I will get rid of it right now." I ran out of the room before he could change his mind. The master shouted something at me, but I moved too quickly to hear but a few words. "Oh Lord, Jesus, Mary and Joseph! Help me!" I whispered as I practically flew down the stairs and out the front door.

"That baby is dead, you hear me!"

I cried as I ran, and Hooney ran after me. "Wait, Hannah! Where you going?" I paused, but only for a moment. I wept as I told her what happened.

"Did you hear him, Hooney? He says this baby is dead. I think he is going to kill her."

"Nothing you can do but take that baby away. The master says that baby is dead, it's dead. Take her somewhere where he can't harm her. I know where you should go—to the doctor! Quick, go now! Follow the road until it forks, then go left like you're going to town. It's the yellow house with the green windows! Go, Hannah!"

The master yelled again, and his voice sounded closer and closer. Oh Lord, he's like the devil chasing me! What will he do to us if he finds us, baby child?

The rain began to fall, but I did not let that slow me. I kept my eyes slitted against the raindrops as I flew down the red clay road. I had to get the baby to a safe place. I had to, for Miss Christine! Imagine someone wanting to kill an innocent baby!

Not tonight. Not if I had anything to say about it!

Chapter Seven

"CJ—Carrie Jo! Wake up! Carrie Jo! Now!" Detra Ann's concerned face hovered over me as she roughly shook my shoulders. "Hey, are you with me, girl?"

"What? Is everything okay? Was I talking in my sleep?"

"Try screaming! You almost gave me a heart attack," she said with a nervous laugh. "I thought the boogeyman was chasing you and..." her voice dropped to a whisper, "I thought I heard something downstairs."

Her cool hands grabbed mine, and I could see in the dim light that her eyes were wide and fearful.

"I'm sure it's nothing. Just me scaring up some nightmares. I apologize, Detra Ann. Let's try to get some sleep. I'll keep quiet now, I promise."

She nodded but didn't move. She was convinced she'd heard something. I glanced at my watch; it was 4:30. We remained quiet, holding hands, waiting for any sound. I felt the hair on my arm prickle up in alarm and anticipation. Yep, something or someone was with us at Seven Sisters.

After a minute, I asked in a whisper, "What did it sound like?"

"Kind of like..." Before Detra Ann could answer, I heard a loud thump coming from the bottom floor. "Like that!" The willowy blonde froze, unsure what to do.

"I heard it too this time." The thump was a footstep. Someone was walking—no, stomping—up the wooden staircase. *Stomp, shuffle, stomp, shuffle…*

"What do we do?"

I slung the covers off and ran to the door as quietly as I could. Yes, I had set the lock, but I was not leaving anything to chance. "Hand me that wooden chair!" Detra Ann did as I asked, and I slid the chair under the doorknob hoping that would protect us.

Stomp, shuffle, stomp.

"Is that Ashland? Is this some kind of joke?"

"What? No!" I whispered furiously. "He doesn't even know we're here—nobody does!" The stomping continued, and the sound was very close to us now.

"Oh my God! It's at the top of the stairs now! What do we do?" Detra Ann was nearly in tears.

I grabbed my phone off the nightstand and dragged her by the hand to the far corner of the room, nearest the window. It was too late to call anyone—the intruder was here with us. The fear mounted as the stomps sounded louder and more threatening. Suddenly, the sound stopped, and I squeezed Detra Ann's hand as fiercely as she squeezed mine. I watched in terror as the doorknob began to turn ever so slowly. I heard Detra Ann gasp. The doorknob turned easily now, more quickly. I was just about ready to call out, to scare away whoever stood outside the door, when I heard a voice growl, "Christine!" I knew that voice—it was Jeremiah

Cottonwood! There would be no reasoning with him—not in this life or any other.

"Oh, hell!" I began to pat the wall frantically. I shoved the phone in the pocket of my pajama pants and searched in the near dark.

"What are you doing?" Detra Ann exclaimed, nearly frightened out of her mind.

"Looking for a door! There has to be a way out of here!"

"There is! Move that picture!"

I lifted the heavy-framed picture off the wall and set it on the floor. The ridge was discernible now, but only barely.

"Christine!" the voice insisted, angry that he could be denied access. The doorknob continued to rattle until the door opened a tiny bit. I heard the wooden chair crack and creak. The phantom paused his assault, and it seemed I could hear him breathing. *But that can't be true! He can't breathe! He's been dead for over a hundred and fifty years!*

"Here!" Detra Ann pushed on the corner of the hidden door, and the latch gave way. A small door, just big enough for one person at a time to fit through opened, and she scurried through. I climbed in behind her, closing the door furiously just in time to hear Christine's bedroom door, the chair or both splinter behind us.

"Run, Detra Ann!" I yelled at her.

I heard her sob, "I can't see!"

I stepped in front of her. "It's okay. I have my phone. Follow me." We began to move quickly. The dust under my feet felt sticky and thick. I held her hand and turned on the flashlight app on my phone so we could work through the stuffy labyrinth. Finally, we came to a short set of stairs. We almost fell down them, but we managed to control our fear long enough to get downstairs without killing ourselves.

Above us, we could hear the stomping grow louder. Thank God, the malevolent ghost of Jeremiah wasn't in here with us. Detra Ann sobbed again, and I tried to comfort her. "It's okay, I promise. We'll be out of here soon."

"If we leave our hiding spot, won't we still be in the house with that thing?"

"Just stay close." At some point during our frantic escape, I hit my mouth. My lip felt swollen, and I could taste blood. Still, I was alive—we were alive! The air smelled stale, but I forced myself to breathe as normally as I could. We walked past another hidden door; I could see an unearthly light shining from behind it. I thought about pushing it open, but a fleeting shadow passed across the light. Nope! Not this one! I couldn't tell where we were—probably somewhere behind the dining hall wall. In the distance, I could hear what sounded like a piano crash and the furious stomping became louder, so loud that it sounded like a freight train. Forget controlling my breathing—it was so hard that my chest hurt; sweat dripped down my face and neck. I dragged Detra Ann behind me and ran on into the dusty darkness. She stumbled as I came to a stop. I flashed my light against the wall. It had to be here somewhere! It had to be! Suddenly, the door popped open without any help from us. We froze on the spot, neither of us breathing or moving. Nothing came. I pushed it open.

We couldn't stay trapped in the wall all night. At any moment Jeremiah Cottonwood could decide to appear, and who or what could stop him? "When we get out, run to the right to the back door. You ready?"

"I don't know, but let's do this." Even in the shadows, I could see the determined look on her face. "Don't you dare let me go!"

"You either!"

I pushed the door open wider. It struck a small side table, slinging picture frames and porcelain pieces to the ground. We were out of the wall and didn't waste time dawdling in the dining room.

"Christine," the disembodied voice growled at us from somewhere near. We couldn't see him, but it was as if he were everywhere at once. Suddenly, the stomping above us stopped but there was another sound coming from the window. A windstorm blew outside, and the branches of the live oaks were slapping at the windows viciously as if they would whip us too. For some reason, it entranced me.

"Don't stop!" Detra Ann yelled at me. It was her turn to drag me now. She ran toward the open door; her ponytail had come undone, and her blond hair flew behind her. I held onto her hand for dear life.

"Christine! You are mine!" I heard the voice yell—Jeremiah's anger was palpable. I slid on the freshly waxed wooden floor of the hallway that led to the back door. I ungracefully sailed against the wall and crashed to the ground, and my knee crunched as I landed. Detra Ann struggled to help me up, and I yelped in pain.

"Run, Detra Ann! Go!"

"I'm not leaving you, so get your ass up—now!" Her adrenaline surging, she practically jerked me up off the ground, snatched my arm and slung it over her shoulder. The green potted palms begin to move under the influence of the unearthly wind. The brochures and flyers that had been so neatly arranged on the welcome table were now scattered about the room. I heard a distinct giggle—a familiar giggle. Then whispered words sent chills deep into my soul: "You'll be worm food now, I suppose!" *Isla! They were both here!*

The massive double doors that led to the back garden seemed so far away, but we awkwardly ran together. I ignored the pain, determined not to hinder Detra Ann from escaping Seven Sisters.

"Oh God—oh God—oh God!" she whispered like a chant. We could feel the supernatural presence surging, swelling behind us like a cloud of evil that threatened to overwhelm us and steal our warm bodies from the land of the living. If we turned to look, I was sure we would see something awful, something we would never forget. There wasn't a chance that I was going to look behind me. I closed my eyes and ran for the door on my damaged knee.

"Keep moving!" I shouted to myself and to Detra Ann, and then my phone began to ring in my pocket. Only it wasn't my ring tone that played—it was the tune from Christine's music box! No way was I going to stop to look and see who called me.

It was my turn to panic. "Oh God!" Somehow, we made it to the back door. I hung on Detra Ann's shoulder as she flipped the dead bolt. This time I did look—I saw Isla hovering against a wall, floating above us, grinning as she watched us fight for our lives. I did not see Jeremiah Cottonwood, but a solid black cloud was moving toward us from the stairway. He was coming! My phone rang nonstop in my pocket; Christine's song played at an unearthly decibel. Suddenly, Detra Ann swung open the door and everything stopped. Isla and the black cloud disappeared. The stomping, the laughter, the wind—it all stopped.

"Come on, CJ! No looking back. Let's go!"

I don't know how we managed it, but we made it to the first cast-iron bench in the Moonlight Garden. It was pitch-black out. The skies were clear, with no storms at all, but the stars had begun to fade. The sun would make its appearance soon. I leaned on Detra Ann's shoulder, trying to catch my breath.

"We're okay. We're alright," she panted, her voice filled with relief. She hugged me and began to cry.

I patted her back to comfort her and finally whispered, "Yes, we are." *Please let this be the end of it!* I reached in my pocket and pulled out my phone.

The message on my screen read: *You Have 2 Missed Calls!* Curious to see what it would say, I tapped on the screen. *Unknown Caller at 5:00 AM.*

We sat staring at the open door, but nothing ever emerged. I didn't know what Detra Ann was thinking, but I was ready for this dream catching experience to be over. My knee was screaming, and my blood was still pumping furiously from our unexpected run through the house.

"Is it always like that?"

"No, it's not, I promise. Or I would lose my mind."

"I'm not sure I haven't lost mine. I don't know how you live with this. Now I see why TD is having such a hard time dealing with his experience."

"It's a rare thing, but it is disturbing when it happens. Something happened tonight, something triggered Jeremiah Cottonwood's anger. He didn't like us in his wife's room."

"Maybe he's worried that you might find another treasure?" I could tell she was doing her best to reason away the spirit's attack.

"Maybe he was—but I don't think so. He wasn't after the treasure; he wanted Christine, remember? He kept calling her. I don't know what just happened. I need time to think."

"So do I! I'm ready to go, but my keys are upstairs. You need to go to the hospital."

"Not me. I'm fine. What about you?" My knee was throbbing, but I didn't want to go anywhere until I was sure we were safe.

"Well, there appears to be only one thing to do."

"Detra Ann—you can't go back in there!"

"No worries, girl. I don't plan on it! The police will be here soon. We tripped the silent alarm when we walked outside without entering the code in the keypad."

"Oh, thank God. Then maybe we can go home. I have had enough fun for one night." I put my arms around her and hugged her. She'd said she wanted to hang out with a dream catcher. Well, be careful what you wish for. Sometimes the dream sticks around and follows you home! I hoped Jeremiah would stay within the confines of Seven Sisters and not show up at my new place as I suspected Isla had been doing.

There had to be something I could do—then I remembered something Henri Devecheaux once told me. "Spirits don't come unless they are welcomed, and they only stay when they have a claim to something. You want to keep a spirit away? Don't welcome it, and don't give it a claim on anything you own."

That might be easier said than done, though. I was beginning to think Isla had her sights set on Ashland.

And alive or dead—she never played by the rules.

Chapter Eight

Thankfully, it wasn't Detective Simmons who responded to the alarm. It must have been too early in the day for her. No doubt if she had heard the call, she would have been here, ready to lick her pencil and give me unbelieving stares. We'd certainly given her enough to think about. That reminded me—I needed to call her about Mia. I felt sure that the woman who tried to kill me shouldn't know my new address, and she sure as heck didn't need to be writing me.

During our ten-minute wait, Detra Ann and I concocted a story to explain why the house was in such a state and why we didn't want to go inside. We'd say a squirrel found its way in the house and we ran out. That might also explain why it looked like a tornado had blown through the downstairs foyer. The officer, an older gentleman, didn't doubt us—he seemed happy to "rescue" two pretty young women from a dangerous rodent. He did a search of the house and declared that whatever animal it was must have made a break for it because the house was all clear.

"That's great, but I'm not staying. If you wouldn't mind, we'll just grab our things and leave."

Officer Thornton looked tired after his sweep. "I can't understand why you were here to begin with. This isn't a residence, is it?"

"We were working late getting some things ready for the Halloween Tour and figured we'd just spend the night. Then that rowdy squirrel came in and liked to have scared us to death." Detra Ann was doing a marvelous job playing her role as the helpless blonde who needed a big strong man to rescue her. I found it funny to say the least.

"Oh, I see. Ended up scaring yourselves silly, did you?"

I could tell by the way Detra Ann's back stiffened that she didn't care for his tone. I smiled and said, "Well, you know how it is in these big old houses. Give us just a minute." We walked up the stairs and gathered our stuff.

"What a jerk!"

"Let's just get out of here. I guess we should change first. I can't drive through Mobile in my pajamas. People think I'm nuts anyway."

"Only Holliday Betbeze," Detra Ann said with a giggle as she pulled on her jeans. "That was quite a speech you gave at the Historical Society. I can't believe you told those women your mother was mentally ill."

"They would have heard about it eventually. I figured why put off the inevitable? I believe in taking charge of my life in every way possible." We didn't bother making the beds or cleaning up the foyer. The clock said 5:30—still too early to be up. I wanted nothing more than to go home and climb into bed with Ashland, but he wasn't there. I didn't want to be alone again, not right now.

As if she'd read my mind, Detra Ann asked, "Want to grab some breakfast? I don't think I'm ready to go home right now."

"Me either. That sounds wonderful." We thanked Officer Thornton, and Detra Ann locked up Seven Sisters again. I wondered what her employees would think when they saw the mess we'd made.

Still a bit jumpy, I rode in my car alone—I refused to leave it on the property. I turned the radio to a boring talk radio station. Just something to keep my mind busy, make me feel normal again. With a sigh, I followed Detra Ann, wondering what we would talk about over breakfast. I didn't know where she was going, and I didn't really care—I just wanted to get away from Seven Sisters. I kept hoping to see the fat orange sun climb above the Mobile Bay. I wanted this night to be officially over! Instead, steel gray clouds shielded the sun, so I was left listening to WPMX for comfort. Mike and Dave were no less boring than usual. I needed boring at the moment.

I turned up the volume, listening to Mike extol the virtues of the new roundabout that the city had installed on Old Government Street. He was making some good points when the radio began to distort. I hit the tune button, but to no avail. "Well, rats." Watching the road with one eye, I tapped on the radio buttons in search of another channel. I felt tired and still a bit freaked out. I switched from the FM radio to the satellite radio, and still nothing. *What? How is that possible? Something should be working.*

Stupidly, I turned up the volume as if that would help.

Help me…

Help me…I can't see…

The voice was faint, almost indiscernible. I turned up the volume again but heard nothing.

"Hello? Is someone there?"

You...help me... You saw me...

Suddenly and with perfect clarity, I knew who was talking to me. It was Christine! We had connected in the dream—somehow, she had seen me. Now here she was being spooky in my radio. Out of sheer fright, I turned off the radio. The light changed and Detra Ann was making a right turn into By the Bay Bed and Breakfast. I pulled into the spot beside her and put the car in park.

What had I done? Why had I gone back to Seven Sisters? Ashland warned me to stay away, but I didn't heed his advice. Now my radio was talking to me and angry ghosts chased me out of the home I'd loved. I laid my tired head on the steering wheel, but I didn't cry. I was too tired to cry.

Detra Ann opened the car door, squatted down beside me and patted my back. A few moments later, she said, "Let's go have some coffee. Hardly anybody comes here, and I know the owner. We can sit on the back porch and look at the water. We don't have to talk if you don't want to. Sound good?"

"Sure." Coffee sounded really good right now. I grabbed my bag and followed her to the back porch dining area. There was an old man sitting at a faraway table reading his Mobile Press Register and drinking coffee. He politely raised his cup to us and then went back to his paper.

A middle-aged woman wearing a Smuckers jam apron walked out on the porch with a pot of coffee and two cups. "Good morning, Detra Ann. Y'all having coffee this morning? You're up awful early."

"Good morning, Gloria. Yes, ma'am, and a basket of biscuits too, please."

"Sure thing. You want those with fig or peach preserves?"

"How about both?"

Our friendly server smiled as if she'd just been told she won the lottery. "Wonderful! I'll be right back." She laid a small laminated menu on our table along with the coffee and cups. Detra Ann poured two steaming cups of black coffee and placed one in front of me.

We sipped for a minute, and the silence was wonderful. Gloria came back with the promised hot biscuits, and I helped myself to one. They smelled buttery and delicious—how could I resist? This was normal, this was what I needed, to drink coffee with a friend. She was a friend, wasn't she? I placed an order for scrambled eggs and bacon, and Detra Ann asked for grits and eggs.

"I heard a voice on the radio," I confessed.

"What? Like a talk show?" Her tired eyes were apprehensive. She had to be thinking I was nuts.

"No, not like a talk show. Something happened in my dream tonight, something that has never happened before. Christine saw me. I think, no, I *know* she knew I was there! She asked me who I was—she thought I was an angel come to take her to heaven!"

"What? That's impossible, CJ."

"No more impossible than dreaming about the past and going back in time! No more impossible than a dead man chasing us out of his house!"

"Don't get mad. This is all new to me. What happened? I mean, how does it normally work? Is it like a vision?"

"I transferred tonight—I saw from different viewpoints. That means instead of being just one person, I was two. There was a girl there, Hannah—she was a young slave. At times, I was looking through her eyes, and at other times I was Christine Cottonwood. It seemed that when they touched, I switched viewpoints, like I was watching a movie. That's never happened before. I wonder what it means."

"I'm dying to know, what did you see?"

"I saw Christine giving birth to a baby, and she didn't even know she was there. Her mind was so fragmented, so fragile. Isla really did a number on her, and so did Jeremiah. I think he'd been abusing his wife to the point that when she heard Louis was dead, she checked out. But that's only a guess right now."

"Checked out how?"

With shaking hands I put another biscuit on a china plate and buttered it. Ooh…I felt dizzy. I realized it had been way too long since I'd eaten.

What a pretty pattern! Blue butterflies dancing around the rim, such a happy dish. I loved butterflies. I had forgotten how much...

"Carrie Jo?"

"What?"

She laughed nervously. "Checked out how?"

"Oh, when I was her, she went from one thing to the next, with no logical train of thought. One minute she was seeing Calpurnia dancing in the corner of the room, and the next she was walking through a garden with her brother. She couldn't have been older than twelve. Next she was... oh my gosh!" I took a sip of my coffee, hardly believing what I was remembering. My brain felt tired—no, sticky, as if there were some type of residue left over from my dream catching. I felt off—weird.

"Christine was *avoir une liaison* with her doctor, and it wasn't just a one-time thing. She was in love with him—she thought of him as her *vrai mari*. Christine loved him more than anyone, except her daughter."

Detra Ann laughed again. "I didn't know you spoke French. You are a girl of hidden talents, Carrie Jo." She smeared peach preserves on a biscuit and popped a piece in her mouth.

I stared at her like she'd slapped me. "I don't speak French. I never have."

"Surely you must. You just spoke it perfectly. Maybe you took a high school or college course?"

"I didn't take French ever. I took Spanish and Latin." We stared at one another.

What a pretty lady. Such vibrant blue eyes, trustworthy eyes. Louis says the eyes are the windows of the soul. Such a poet he is!

What was happening to me? I clutched my napkin like it was a life preserver and I was drowning.

"Well, you must have heard Christine speaking French and the words stuck in your brain. That makes sense— well, as much sense as any of this does. Hey, are you okay?"

"I…uh…yeah. I'm fine."

"So Christine and her doctor? That's kind of scandalous, especially for those days. Tell me what you know."

Hoyt! Where are you, Hoyt?

Oh my God! I am going nuts! I should have listened to Ashland. I should never have gone back to Seven Sisters. What was I thinking? …Hoyt?

I practically leapt out of my chair. "Detra Ann, thank you for breakfast, but I think I better go home. I'm tired and my mind is racing…"

"Aw, but we're just getting to the good part."

I reached for my bag. She was chewing on her biscuit, and I could see our food approaching. I couldn't stay— I couldn't have a meltdown here in the middle of this nice bed and breakfast.

"I'm sorry. I'll call you later." I stumbled trying to get off the porch but I kept on walking. *I have to go home…take me home!*

Detra Ann followed me to the car. She was talking to me, but my ears weren't listening. I felt tired, ready to go to sleep. *Yes, maybe a nap would calm my nerves. Calpurnia…come lie down with Mother.*

"Carrie Jo? Let me come with you. You don't look well."

"Je vais bien," I lied with a smile, feigning happiness, "really I am."

"But you just…"

"Please, let me get some rest and I will call you later. I promise." I closed the door and pulled out of the gravel parking lot. As I turned on to the side road, I glanced at myself in the mirror. Yes, I was still Carrie Jo Jardine Stuart, but there was something else going on behind those green eyes. I couldn't see her, but I knew she was there.

Now it all made sense. Why Jeremiah chased us through the house! Why he tried so desperately to stop us from leaving! She had made her escape through me! She had been with us the whole time, and her husband knew it.

Somehow, Christine Beaumont Cottonwood had returned, but why? And for how long? How would this end?

This time, I really had gone too far.

Chapter Nine

Carrie Jo drove away, kicking up rocks from the back tires of her tan Cadillac. She sped out of the parking lot without even a courtesy wave. *Ashland is going to kill me!* I walked back to the porch and made excuses to Gloria about why my friend took off so suddenly. "She's not been feeling well. This looks delicious!" I smiled and Gloria walked away, happy that at least I was staying to enjoy her home-cooked breakfast.

I took my phone out of my purse and stared at it as I poured myself another cup of coffee. What was I going to say to him?

Sorry. I had a sleepover at Seven Sisters with your wife, and now she's gone a little nuts.

No. That wasn't true. She believed what she told me about her dream catching. That much I was sure of. CJ had her secret power, but I had one too. Well, a couple actually. I was a human lie detector. Whenever someone lied to me, big or small, bells went off. Carrie Jo didn't have an inch of dishonesty in her—not until she told me everything was okay. In general, she had a unique honesty about her, but now my "bells" were ringing like crazy. She wasn't okay, and that was partially my fault.

Ashland had asked me to befriend his wife and help her get to know our circle of friends. But with everything going south with TD, and with the added responsibility of my sick mother, I just hadn't gotten around to it. I'd had every intention of hosting a party for the new couple or something, but then I got started on the Halloween Ball. At least Carrie Jo had promised to attend. That would be the perfect time to present her to everyone…if we got that far. I wasn't sure she'd ever want to step into Seven Sisters again—me either for that matter. I didn't know what happened with her dreams, except the little she told me. But what happened afterwards, that was completely real.

In just about an hour, I would call Rachel Kowalski and give her a heads up on the mess we had left behind. I planned to use the invading squirrel defense, the same as we had with the cop. Hopefully she wouldn't ask too many questions.

It was early, but I called Ashland. He needed to know what happened. I figured I might as well fess up and get it over with. "Hey, did I wake you?"

"Of course not. What's up?"

"It's Carrie Jo."

"What is it? Is she okay?" I could hear the desperation in his voice, which made me feel even guiltier. What kind of friend was I? So far, he'd proven to be a better friend to me than I had been to him. I would never forget what he did for me—how he stayed by my side after Fred Price assaulted me. He was there every step of the way, and I could never repay him. I had five brothers, but Ashland had proven to be a better brother than any of them. It was too bad we didn't have romantic feelings for one another. According to my mother, we should have skipped the love part.

"Love can come after marriage, Detra Ann," she'd said. "Compatibility is much more important to a happy marriage."

I had replied, "Not for me. One day, I'll fall madly in love and that will be it." I knew the truth—she wasn't actually concerned about my happiness. The only thing she truly cared about was where our family ranked on the city's "Most Wealthy" list. My marriage to Ashland Stuart would have permanently secured for her the top spot, right over the head of Holliday Betbeze. *Sorry, Mom. I'm not going to use my friend to help you get a better parking spot and boost your ego—or your bank account.*

"Yes, she is fine—at least I think she is. She came to the house last night, Ash, to Seven Sisters."

"What? Why?"

"I think she wanted to talk about TD, but then I made a mistake. Don't be mad, but I let her stay there last night."

"Are you crazy? That's the last thing she needs!"

"For the record, you never told me to lock her out! Besides, I was with her. As much as I love you, I'm not your wife's keeper!" The old man across the porch gave me an irritated glare and then turned the page of his newspaper, pretending that he wasn't listening.

He sighed heavily into the phone. "What makes you think she's not okay? What happened? She had a dream?"

In a whisper I told him, "Yes, but the real strangeness didn't happen until after she woke up. I think she brought something back with her. We got chased out of the house this morning—whatever it was nearly tore the place up. We got out okay, but it was the weirdest thing I have ever experienced. This ghost—this entity, it was after us, Ashland. After her, I think. I thought she was handling it all well. I mean, I'm the one that should be freaking out—I had no idea this would happen. But then it just went wrong. I took her to breakfast, and that's when she went all strange."

"Strange how?"

I gestured wildly with my hands, as if he could see me. "All daydreamy and confused. And another thing…does she know French?"

"No, I don't think so. We were just in Haiti, and she never spoke it there."

"She's speaking French."

"What?"

"I can't be sure, but I think she's kind of losing it, you know, mentally. Did you know that her mother is mentally ill? She told the entire Historical Society, Ash."

"I know all about Carrie Jo, and she's no crazier than you or I. Where is she now, Detra Ann?"

"I took her to breakfast at Gloria's place, but she went home before our food arrived. She should be there now. You should call her."

"I've been trying! Now I know why she hasn't been answering. I need you to go there and stay with her until I get home. Please don't leave her alone. If you can't go, then I can call Bette. I'm on the way, and I can be there in an hour and a half—two at the most."

I poked at my eggs with my fork and leaned back in the wicker chair. "Fine. I'll go, but I'd like to go home and change first. And when you get home, we've got to talk about that house. How am I supposed to go back there now?"

"Don't wait, please. I need you to go now."

"What am I supposed to say to her? 'Please let me in— your husband sent me over to spy on you?'"

"No, but you can tell her that I heard she wasn't feeling good and that I asked you to come over. It's the truth—she hasn't been taking my calls, and I *am* worried about her. We've not been…well, we have had some problems lately."

My heart sank a little. Carrie Jo had hinted at this. I wanted Ashland to be happy—I knew he cared for Carrie Jo a great deal—probably more than anyone else I'd seen him with. For goodness' sake, he married her.

"Okay, I'll do it. Be safe. I'll see you there."

I hung up and finished off my breakfast. I sent Rachel a super long text about the "squirrel" and explained that I would be coming in late. She sent back an "Okay" and that was that. I was sure she'd light up my phone after she saw what had taken place inside. Then what would I say?

Yeah, sorry about the mess the stark-raving ghost left us. Try not to upset him, and don't mention the name Christine.

Gloria picked up my plates, and I gathered my belongings. I paid the bill and drove to Carrie Jo's house. Unfortunately, I was behind a street cleaning truck that refused to get out of the way. I knew he saw me waving at him, but he still didn't budge.

"This is just great," I complained to the truck. My phone rang and started singing "Thank God I'm a Country Boy." I knew it was TD. I couldn't dig the phone out of my purse fast enough. We hadn't spoken in weeks, and our last conversation wasn't anything nice. I'd given him an ultimatum and he gave me his answer—I came home to find all his things gone. I'd cried all night but hadn't called him. He had not called me either.

"Hey!" I said as casually as I could while juggling the phone and the steering wheel. *Keep your game face on, girl, and don't get wimpy!*

"Hey, beautiful." I loved his warm voice, and I especially loved it when he called me that. He had a delicious Southern accent that made him sound uber-sexy. His accent was distinct and fine in a way that set him apart from the other guys around here. He could talk excitedly about projects and buildings, but when it came to him and me—he was slow and on purpose. I'd loved that.

"Good to hear from you, TD. How have you been?" *Be cool, be aloof!*

"Things are good and getting better—especially now that I am talking to you. I have so much to say to you, beautiful. I was hoping we might have coffee this morning—if you'd be willing to see me. I know I have been wrong about so much—I would like to apologize and talk about our future—if you think we might have one."

Uh-oh, something doesn't feel right. Probably just some apprehension left over from last night. So why is my "lie detector" going off like crazy?

"I would like that, but I have to visit a sick friend this morning. I am going to go check on her now. I'll be available in a few hours. Is that okay?"

"Yes, we could meet later this morning, if you have some time for me."

"Are you sure you are okay, TD?"

He chuckled. It sounded insincere, kind of forced. "Never better! Just can't wait to see your gorgeous face." *He was lying to me—but about what?*

"Alright… so where should we meet?"

"Why don't you come to my place? I would like to talk somewhere private, talk things over, see what I can do to make it up to you. I know I've been a jerk."

Nope. This is a bad idea.

"I think I would like to take things a bit slower. Can we meet at Starbucks, the one on Airport?"

"Alright. I'll be there. See you at ten?"

"Okay, I'll see you then."

"Detra Ann?"

"Yes?"

"Thanks for agreeing to see me."

"See you later, TD." I hung up the phone, caught a break in the traffic and whizzed around the truck. If I weren't such a lady, I would have given that guy a piece of my mind—or at least an ugly gesture. When I got to Carrie Jo's house, her shiny new car was in the driveway. I pulled the BMW up behind it and wondered what I would say to her.

Why am I here? If something creepy is going on, I'm out of here. I can't take another creepy thing! I don't even believe in ghosts!

I dropped my keys in my purse and slung it over my shoulder. I hoped this wouldn't take too long. All I had to do was check on her and ask her to call Ashland.

"Oh no," I said to myself when I walked up the sidewalk. The front door stood wide open, and dead magnolia leaves from the front yard had blown into the house. This didn't look right—not one little bit. I stood on the pavement wondering what to do next. Visions of my own attack five years ago flashed in my head. I practically ran to the open door. "Carrie Jo?" There wasn't a sound in return except the sound of rustling leaves. I hadn't noticed the breeze until now—it picked up a swirl of dry leaves and tossed them around the foyer. She wasn't answering, and I couldn't leave here until I knew she was okay. I just couldn't.

I stepped into the foyer, a layer of leaves crunching under my feet. I continued to call her name, when I heard a sound from upstairs and froze in my tracks. Oh my God! What if someone else was here—an attacker like Fred Price? I dug in my purse for my tiny pearl-handled gun. I wasn't taking any chances. This could be a dangerous area at times—I mean, I loved Mobile, but we had our share of violent criminals. I walked through the entire lower hallway and checked all the rooms as if I were a rookie police officer.

"Carrie Jo?" I said again, this time in a whisper. I heard another sound—definitely coming from upstairs. She could be hurt up there; I had no choice but to climb those stairs. I left my bag on the lower steps and began to work my way up. *Thank God I'm not wearing my usual high heels today.* Between the leaves and the wooden steps whoever was up there, if anyone at all, would know I was coming long before I got there.

I called her name again. This time I plainly heard a door close. The sound wasn't too far away either. I gritted my teeth and kept moving up. I was just three steps from the top now. *Not too late to change your mind. Go outside and call the police.* I stopped and lowered my gun. Maybe that was what I should do. What was I thinking? How was I qualified to do this? Just because I had once been a victim didn't mean I was now an expert. Before I could sneak back down, the door closest to me opened and out walked Carrie Jo in a terry robe with a towel wrapped around her head. She jumped back in surprise, and suddenly I felt a cruel punch in my gut. My gun flew out of my hand. I could hear the sound of the shot.

I screamed as the sensation of falling overwhelmed me. My arms reached out for something, anything, to help me stop my fall, but I couldn't grasp a hold of the rail. I heard a loud pop, then a thud, and everything went dark.

Chapter Ten

"Detra Ann!" I screamed in horror as I scrambled down the stairs after the fallen blonde. Blood poured out of her side, and the smell of gunpowder filled the air. I hadn't touched her but she'd fallen somehow. "Detra Ann!" I screamed and ran to her side. I squatted next to her in the blood and felt for a pulse. She was alive—at least for now.

Doreen walked inside and stifled a yell behind her hands. "Oh my God! Oh my God!"

"Doreen! Call 911, now! Please!"

She dropped her grocery bags on the floor and ran for the phone. "Yes, we have an emergency." She handed me the phone and ran to get towels for Detra Ann, who was still unconscious.

"Yes! I need help. My friend fell down the stairs. She was carrying a gun, and I think she's been shot. Please come! She's bleeding pretty bad. Please help us."

"Okay, ma'am. They are on the way. It won't be but a minute. Is she breathing? Can you see?"

"Yes, but it's shallow."

"Okay, now you say she's been shot?"

"Yes, oh my God! Please hurry!"

"Where has she been shot?"

"In the side, around her waist. I think she lost control of the gun as she fell. I don't know! Oh my God! She's my friend, but she's not supposed to be here. I came out of the bathroom and she was here."

"It's okay. Don't worry about that right now. Let's see if we can stop the bleeding. Do you have some towels?" asked the friendly dispatcher.

"Yes, I do now."

"Fold a towel and press it to the area where's she been shot. That should slow down any blood loss."

"Make them hurry! She's bleeding through the towel. Please, Detra Ann. Don't you dare die!"

I could hear the ambulance tearing down Government Street. Doreen scrambled to her feet and opened the door and then ran to the laundry room.

"Detra Ann, stay with me! Can you hear me?"

Her dark eyelashes fluttered, but she never opened her eyes completely. I saw her body sag just as the EMTs came barging in the front door.

"What happened?"

"I don't know. I think she tripped and fell—her gun went off. I didn't even know she had a gun! She's been shot." I got out of the way as the two young men squatted down beside her.

"What's her name?"

"Detra Ann. Please, is she going to be alright?"

"We'll do our best to help her."

I watched as they assessed her quickly and prepared her for transport. They braced her neck and expertly moved her body to the gurney.

"Here, ma'am. I got you some clothes." Doreen handed me a tote bag with a shirt, jeans, underwear and sandals.

"Thank you. Please call Mr. Stuart for me. Tell him to come to the hospital."

"I will!"

I followed the men to the ambulance and didn't wait for an invitation to join them. I climbed inside and sat out of the way on the only available metal bench. While working furiously to stop the bleeding they asked me questions about allergies and blood type. I didn't know what to tell them—I didn't know any of these things. The sight of Detra Ann near death, her normally tanned face pale and lifeless, sent shockwaves through my psyche. What had she been doing in my house? How did she get in, and why did she have a gun? I couldn't answer any of those questions but whatever the answer, I prayed that she would live. The rest of the ride was a blur. When we arrived at the hospital, I ran after the gurney. The EMTs paused in the ER hallway only long enough to call for a doctor. "She's bleeding out! Code Six!" They whirred past me through a set of self-locking doors. I wanted to chase them into the operating room, but a sympathetic nurse blocked my way.

"I'll meet you at the registration area in a couple of minutes. In the meantime, you can change. There are some scrubs in here," she said kindly, pointing to a nearby closet.

"Thanks, but I have clothes. Is there a bathroom I can use?"

"Right through there." She hurried away, following after Detra Ann and the team that had assembled around her. I couldn't stop shaking. I stumbled into the bathroom and changed my clothes quickly. Fortunately for me, Doreen had enough foresight to include my cell phone. What a relief!

With shaking fingers, I called Ashland. Strangely enough, he was already on the line. He'd been trying to call me. I let out a sob. "Baby? Are you there?"

"Yes, Carrie Jo. Are you okay? Doreen called me. What have they told you about Detra Ann?"

"I'm fine. I'm at the hospital, Springhill. They haven't said much yet. They just took her back. Are you on the way?" I was in full-blown crying mode now.

"I am—I'll be there in about an hour. Do you have someone with you? Maybe Bette?"

"No, I'll be fine." I scurried out of the bathroom and went in search of the nurse at the registration desk. "I have to go. The nurse wants to talk with me. I don't know what to tell her."

"I'll call Cynthia and tell her to get down there. She can answer their questions. Just take a deep breath, and I'll be there soon."

"Ashland?"

"Yes?"

"Hurry, please."

"I will. I'll talk to you soon."

He hung up, and I stood at the registration desk waiting for the nurse. When she didn't return I called Terrence Dale. He didn't answer, so I left him a message. "Hey, this is Carrie Jo. I'm calling because Detra Ann is at Springhill. She's had an accident, and I think it might be a good idea for you to be here. I'm in the emergency waiting room. Bye." Fifteen minutes later, I took a seat in the waiting room, hoping that the nurse would come back eventually.

The first person to arrive was TD. Detra Ann was right, he did look different. He was thinner now, and his silky brown hair brushed his shoulders. Not an unattractive look, just different. Even his clothing style had evolved. Now the young contractor wore torn blue jeans and a vintage T-shirt with the emblem of an old rock band on the chest. No more khakis and polo shirts, I supposed. "TD!" I said, throwing my arms around his neck. He tentatively hugged me and awkwardly stepped back.

"What's happened?"

"I'm not sure, really. I came out of the shower, and she was there on the stairs with a gun. I don't know if I startled her or what, but she fell and the gun went off. Now she's shot! In the side! I'm waiting and waiting, but nobody will tell me anything."

"She tried to shoot you?"

"No! I don't think so—I don't know what she was doing, but she is hurt really bad. I witnessed the whole thing, but it all happened so fast. I can't tell you much about what happened."

He hugged me again and helped me find a seat. He said, "Wait here. I'll go see what I can find out."

I watched him chat with the receptionist. She nodded and smiled at him, and he waved at me. "Thank you," he said to her when she pressed the button to let us back. "She's in surgery, but they're allowing us to sit in the surgery waiting room. The doctor will come speak to us when he's finished."

"Oh God! Ashland is on his way in from New Orleans. He said he would call her mother. I haven't heard anything else." We shuffled through the bleach-scented halls of Springhill Memorial until we came to the surgery waiting room.

"Yeah, she knows—she called me too. She was in Foley—she'll be here in about 45 minutes." He plopped down beside me. "The woman hates me. I can't say that I blame her. Detra Ann was way too good for me. Damn—that's her calling me now. Excuse me." He stepped just outside the door and took the call.

With a growing numbness, I sat in the smaller, colder waiting room. There were only a couple of people there. I stared absently at the muted television and waited for TD to return. He came back looking somber—it had been a long time since I'd seen him smile.

"I was supposed to meet her this morning. She said her friend was sick—she was going to check on her and then meet me afterwards. I can't believe this." His head was in his hands, his shoulders slumped. "I've been such a jackass," his voice broke in a sob.

I must have been the sick friend she was referring to. Still, that didn't explain why Detra Ann was in my house with a loaded gun. I knew I had locked that front door, but the hallway was full of leaves again. *I wonder if…I can't figure this out right now!*

"I'm listening." I put a hand on his back as he cried. This was what he needed—he needed to talk. "It's okay—Detra Ann is strong. She'll survive this."

After a few minutes, he stopped crying, and a kind nurse stopped by with a bottle of water and some tissues. "Anything yet?" he asked. "The patient is Detra Ann Dowd."

"No sir. She's still in surgery, but the doctor will come right out when he's finished. If y'all need anything, I'm right outside."

"Thank you."

"TD, I know this is none of my business, and you can tell me to shut up if you like, but what happened? With you and Detra Ann? She's just crazy about you."

"She didn't tell you?" I could see the shame in his brown eyes.

"Well, I heard a little, but I'd like to hear it from you."

"I really don't want to talk about it."

"We don't have to. I'm sorry I asked."

Leaning back in the plastic chair, he sighed. "No, I said I wasn't going to do that anymore. I'm facing my demons. I promised Detra Ann that I had changed. I can't drink away what I saw—what I know I saw." He rubbed his eyes and looked at me. "For a long time I hated you and Ashland—you know, for that night. It was like from that night forward everything went wrong, and I do mean everything. I couldn't focus—tools came up missing—I even got robbed. I lost jobs—I think I lost my mind for a while—a long while."

"I'm truly sorry, TD. I never meant for any of that to happen. I guess I—we didn't count the costs before we went looking for Calpurnia and the treasure. I really am sorry."

"I believe you. I meant to tell Detra Ann something today, but I guess it's not her I'm meant to tell. It's you."

I turned sideways in the chair, my arm on the back, my hand under my chin. "What is it?"

"When I was in high school, my sophomore year, I was in a car accident on I-65. I'd been dating this girl—Ashley Dubose was her name. Sweet girl. We hadn't been dating long, but I was crazy about her. You know, like you are in the tenth grade. One Friday night, we drove downtown to the Saenger Theater to see *Gone with the Wind*, her favorite film. She lived in Theodore, so after the film I took the interstate to get her home faster. Her dad was strict about her curfew, but I didn't mind. I liked her a lot. Everything was great. She was chattering on about Scarlett O'Hara—I was half listening when she kissed my cheek to thank me for taking her. I half-turned to kiss her and took my eyes off the road for only a second. That split second changed everything."

"What happened?"

"A truck sideswiped us and we went spinning. Ashley died. I walked away from the accident with just a scratch on my arm."

"I'm sorry. That must have been so difficult to process."

"It was, but it only got worse. For the next six months, I saw Ashley everywhere I went. Not like a face in a crowd or someone that looked like her. It was her, bleeding, with her empty eyes that stared through me— just like she looked in the car, you know, afterwards. I felt like a crazy person. Imagine sitting in economics class and your dead girlfriend is standing in the corner of the room. Only no one else can see her—just you. Just staring and bleeding. It happened every day for months."

"That sounds horrible. How did you cope?"

"My parents tried every way they could to help me. They're nice people. Medication, grief counseling, therapy—nothing worked. Finally, one afternoon my grandmother picked me up. It had been a rough weekend—it had gotten so bad I didn't want to leave the house. Not even for school. Anyway, Granny Kaye came over one day—she knew all about what I'd been going through. She didn't tell me where we were going or anything. We pulled into the parking lot of Valhalla

Cemetery, and she grabbed my hands and started praying for me. When she was done, she handed me a note card and a pen. She told me to write Ashley a note. I thought that was a crazy idea, but she was adamant. I wrote five words: *I'm sorry. I loved you.* We took the card and some flowers to Ashley's grave." He took a deep breath and continued, "She told me to read it out loud, and I did. I cried the whole time, but I read it. I left the card and the flowers on the grave, and I didn't see Ashley ever again after that. Granny and I never talked about it for the rest of her life, but I will always be grateful for what she did."

"Wow, that is incredible. It must have been so terrifying to see her over and over again like that. I'm glad you had some resolution, though."

"I did until that night in the Moonlight Garden."

"Oh my gosh! You mean she came back?"

"No, it was the other one that I saw, the one that was reaching out for Ashland. Isla, I think her name was."

I shivered and nodded. "You saw her? Where?"

"Everywhere. And worse. Sometimes…"

"What? What is it?"

"Sometimes I'd wake up and she'd be on top of me. I'd scream, and she would disappear. I think I scared Detra Ann to death. She thought I was having nightmares, but they weren't like nightmares. CJ—they were real. She visited me, and I didn't want her to. She was really there, just like Ashley. Only I could smell her, feel her…even taste her. And when I fought her, she would change and I would be kissing a dead thing. I wanted to die. My soul was dying. Anyway, that's when I started drinking. I thought if I was drunk I wouldn't see her. It worked for a little while."

"I am so sorry. I had no idea that you were going through that." Impulsively, I put my arms around his neck and hugged him.

"The problem is I am still going through it, and I don't know what to do."

"Why didn't you tell us? We're your friends, TD. We care about you. Ashland and I would never let you fight her by yourself."

"What does she want? I don't have Granny Kaye in my corner this time, unless you believe in heaven and such. I know she did. She was a praying woman, and I've never been much for faith and prayer. Detra Ann tried to help me, just like Granny Kaye, but she couldn't. She didn't know what to do, and she has no idea about Ashley…" His voice dropped to a whisper. "Or that Isla is lurking around. I can't blame her for dumping me. I am a mess! I don't blame her, and I don't blame you, Carrie Jo."

"Now I know, and together we can fight her. We will figure out why this is happening! Believe it or not, I think I've seen her too." I admitted to TD something I hadn't been ready to tell my own husband. *What am I doing?* "I think she's been at my house."

His brown eyes widened in surprise. "What do you mean?"

"Well, I found this package in my house. It's Mia's handwriting. It was in my house for a month, and there is no way that Ashland or I would have missed it. Isla made sure I found it. I guess it was her. Something did, anyway." I chewed on my lip remembering the shadow that sailed past my door. "I opened the envelope, and inside was a small book—a collection of biographies, but the main story was about an actress named Delilah Iverson."

"I've never heard of her."

"Me either. I haven't finished reading it yet, so I'm not sure how it fits in. That's the kind of thing Isla would do. Death hasn't slowed her down. But besides that unexpected package, I keep seeing someone move out of the corner of my eye. If I am alone in my house, she sails past my door and I hear her giggle. It's bone-chilling." I shivered with the memory.

"I know that feeling," he said. "Yes, it is."

"She's been leaving my front door open and scattering leaves everywhere too. I don't know what to do about her. When Ashland comes home, I guess we'll all be having a 'come to Jesus meeting' because *she* is affecting us all. And there's more…"

Before I could tell him what I knew about Hoyt and Christine, we were interrupted.

"Isn't this cozy? So happy that you two found my daughter's surgery so unimportant that you can't behave respectably."

"What?" TD and I stared at Cynthia Dowd in surprise. She didn't elaborate on her accusations.

Ignoring TD, she addressed me coldly, "How are you, Mrs. Stuart? How is your mother? I hear she's ill."

The gossip from the Historical Society luncheon had traveled quickly. Well, what of it? I had nothing to hide, and I wasn't going to be cowed by my friend's overbearing mother. Before I could open my mouth to speak, the ginger-haired Detective Simmons joined us. She was dressed in a poorly fitting pantsuit with a gaudy pin at the lapel and wore no makeup except some feeble attempts at mascara and an overabundance of lipstick. She was a sharp contrast to the well-dressed Cynthia with her perfect bob cut, Mary Kay makeup and a trim yellow suit. If the difference in statuses bothered the detective, she didn't show it. As usual she pulled out a notebook and a small pencil.

"Just the person I was looking for—Mrs. Stuart. May I talk to you for a minute?"

"Can't it wait, Detective? I am in the middle of a conversation here."

"Suit yourself. We can either talk here or talk down on Government Street in the squad room." She wasn't messing about today. It was her way or the highway apparently.

"Fine, if you'll excuse me, Mrs. Dowd, TD." Only TD acknowledged me.

I followed her down the hall and saw that she was intending to walk out of the hospital. "Where are we going?"

"To my office. Like I said, we need to talk."

"You gave me a choice—I chose to talk to you here. I have no intention of leaving Detra Ann right now. She had an accident, in case you didn't know." I didn't mean to sound snappy, but the abrasive detective had caught me at the wrong moment.

She turned around and stared at me, her pencil in her hand. "In your house! You think I don't know what happens on my beat? I know everything. Would you care to tell me how she got shot in your house?"

"I don't know exactly, or why she was even there. As far as I knew, she had stayed behind to finish her breakfast at By the Bay Bed and Breakfast. I hadn't invited her over."

"So she just broke in and shot herself?" Simmons said with a smirk.

"No, not exactly. After I got home, I went upstairs to take a shower. I needed to relax. When I walked out of the bathroom, Detra Ann was walking up my stairs with her gun drawn. She lost her balance, fell backward and down the steps. As she fell, the gun went off. That was it. That's all I know."

"That seems a bit farfetched, don't you think?"

"I can't help that, Detective. It's the truth."

"You say this woman is your friend?"

"Yes, she is. We've been—we've been working on a project together. I like her, and I am sure the feeling is mutual. She isn't dangerous!"

"You have a hard time keeping friends from killing you, don't you?"

"What?" I stared at her incredulously. I knew what she meant. Mia had tried to kill me, so why not Detra Ann? But I knew Detra Ann would never harm me. Even if we weren't besties, she loved Ashland—I was sure of that.

"It's the truth. People you hang around have a nasty way of getting killed, Miss Jardine—I mean, Mrs. Stuart. Now I want you to come downtown to take a test."

"What kind of test?"

"The kind that tests your hands for gunshot residue. That way, we'll know what happened. It would be a good way to clear your name, ma'am." She raised an eyebrow and scrutinized me.

"What's going on here?" I looked over to see Ashland beside me. I could smell his expensive cologne and felt his warm hand rest gently on my shoulder. "My wife isn't taking any kind of test unless our lawyer says so. Here's her card. Now if you'll excuse us, we have a friend who needs us."

I wanted to kiss him for being there, for coming to my rescue, but I had no reason to run. I knew I was innocent—if I could quickly prove it, why wouldn't I? "Wait, Ashland. I don't mind taking that test. I never fired that gun. I never touched it. If it will clear me, I will do it."

"That's not necessary, CJ. You don't have to do it."

"No, I want to. If it helps the detective, I don't mind. May I come down after I see Detra Ann? She's in surgery right now. I don't know how long that will be."

She nodded begrudgingly. "Sure, that will be fine." She scribbled something on a piece of notebook paper and handed the note to me. "Present this to the officer at the front desk when you get there. They'll get you to the place you need to be. Just walk in and take the test. They wipe your hands with a special cloth, and you wait for the results. They'll know if you fired a gun. If you fired that gun or handled it after it was fired, you will have residue on your hands. If that's the case, you will be arrested."

"Hey…" Ashland started to protest. "She's cooperating, detective."

"No, it's okay. I haven't done anything. I didn't touch that gun! Not before—not afterwards—and sure as heck not during! I will come down soon, Detective. Thank you."

"Fine. Since the patient is in surgery, I can't interview her, but I will send the team to check her hands too. Y'all have a good evening now."

We shook our heads as she left. "What is she thinking?" Ashland asked. "That you would try to kill Detra Ann? What kind of theory is she working? If she had bothered to ask, she would know that I sent Detra Ann to the house. She'd called me and told me you were upset."

"Really? But why did she have her gun out?"

"I don't know. She must have thought something was going on inside—she must have thought you were in danger."

I thought about the door standing wide open. How many times had that happened in the past twenty-four hours? And Ashland didn't even know about it. I decided right then and there that I was going to come clean with him as soon as we were alone. He needed to know that I hadn't been dreaming, until last night, that I'd been seeing Isla and that TD had seen her too. This wasn't over—it seemed the house wasn't through with us yet. But for now, I had to push it aside.

"I don't know, but I am so glad you are here. TD is here, and so is Detra Ann's mother."

"Detra Ann told me what you two did. That you stayed at Seven Sisters. Is that why you weren't answering my calls and why you kept hanging up on me?"

"I only hung up once, and that was because I couldn't hear you. I didn't know you called me."

"How is that possible? I called you like six times, Carrie Jo."

"I don't know what to say except I never got a call from you."

We walked back in silence toward the surgery waiting room. More and more I believed that something was trying to keep us apart—trying to destroy us all. *Oh my God! I am crazy like my mother!*

"When did Mrs. Dowd get here?"

"Just a few minutes ago. I gather she thinks I am involved in the shooting. She made some snide comment about my mother. I guess she heard about my speech at the society lunch."

"I've been meaning to talk to you. You know, your family history is your own business. Why did you open yourself up for ridicule like that?"

"I don't know. Because they are a bunch of busy bees that love to gossip? I figured they would find out the truth anyway, so why not be straight about it. Holliday Betbeze led the pack on that. I'm sorry if I embarrassed you."

"Stop that, Carrie Jo. It's like you don't even know me. I never said you embarrassed me. You've seen how warped and twisted my family is—haven't you?"

"Ashland, I wasn't raised in your kind of world." We stopped in the hallway outside the waiting room. "Where I come from, you tell it like it is. There's no sense in prettying things up. My mother is mentally ill. End of discussion. They kept poking me about her, and I told them. That's it."

He sighed and went in the waiting room. I followed behind him and tried to hide my frustration. *We really are in trouble, aren't we?* Well, at least he came. He was here with me. Or maybe he just came to see Detra Ann.

No matter, he was here. And that meant the world to me.

The pieces were beginning to fall into place. Isla was on the move, and she wanted something from TD. I wondered what the trickster had in mind. And I wondered if, once and for all, I could actually defeat her.

Chapter Eleven

When we left the hospital a few hours later, Detra Ann was sleeping peacefully. The surgeon said she had been very lucky. The bullet had missed her major organs, and there were no fragments left behind. However, she had to be watched the next twenty-four hours. She had lost a lot of blood and had a history of bad reactions to anesthesia.

Mrs. Dowd had appeared genuinely happy that Ashland had come to see her. She'd tolerated TD and me, which was fine with both of us. Ashland tried to include us, but Cynthia had made up her mind to hate us, at least for the moment. After a while, none of us spoke. We sat waiting and staring at Detra Ann, who slept through the whole uncomfortable exchange.

We said our goodbyes, and TD promised to call when she woke up. Ashland still didn't want me to take the gunshot residue test, but I had to. I was innocent! I wanted to prove them all wrong. The faster I was cleared, the more quickly Simmons would start looking at other scenarios. A dull worry began to creep up within me...what if Isla was responsible? I knew she had been there—the open door and the scattered leaves attested to that. Who would ever believe it? The only person who could tell us what really happened was Detra Ann, and she wasn't awake yet.

We drove in silence down Government Street to the Mobile Police Department Headquarters. The only sound was the radio playing softly.

Wait, I know that voice. It was William Bettencourt singing "The Heart of Love." I couldn't help but smile. He deserved the break. I was happy for him. I hummed along to the tune.

"Seriously, CJ?"

"I'm happy that he got his big break."

"Thanks to you. He almost got you killed. I'm not convinced he was so squeaky clean. If he hadn't gotten his name in the papers…"

"That's completely unfair. He saved my life, Ashland." Neither of us moved out of our seats. "I love you, Ashland Stuart. Not William or anyone else."

"I love you too. You ready?" Ashland appeared nervous, unsure. I hoped that his doubts weren't about me. Surely he didn't believe that I actually shot Detra Ann.

"Yes, I want to get this over with and go home. It's been one heck of a day."

"You know I can call our attorney and have her down here in no time."

"I don't need an attorney, Ash. I haven't done anything wrong."

"That doesn't always matter. We have been on the local authorities' radar recently, what with Hollis' murder and Louis Beaumont's body in the backyard. They aren't exactly in our fan club."

I knew it was true, but we were innocent of wrongdoing. We parked, put some change in the meter and walked in, hand and hand. I explained to the on-duty officer why I was there and showed her the written order from Simmons. She led us to the lab and there we sat, taking in the stark ambiance until the lab tech and a uniformed officer appeared. I couldn't help but notice that the police officer had his cuffs handy. True to her word, Simmons wasn't taking any chances. If she could arrest me, she would—she'd promised me that. Now it was my turn to look at Ashland nervously. I gave the tech my name, and then they proceeded with the test. Unsealing the small damp cloth from the package, she rubbed my hands vigorously, both tops and bottoms.

"I'll be right back," she told the officer. He let her pass and stood by the door, his arms folded across his chest. We didn't make any small talk with him or even with each other. It was a nerve-wracking experience to say the least.

"She's clean. Not even a trace." She wrote something on a piece of paper and handed it to me. "Detective Simmons will be in touch with you soon. Keep this for your records."

"That's it? I can go?"

"The detective may have more questions later, but we're all done with you today, Mrs. Stuart."

"Okay."

"If you all would follow me, I'll lead you out." I had had no idea that the entry doors had been locked behind us. Suddenly, the whole thing seemed surreal.

Actually, the past forty-eight hours had been surreal. We walked back to the car and got in. I leaned back in the seat and let out a sigh of relief. Lightning cracked over the bay, and the sky darkened ominously above us.

"Take me home, Ashland." I felt so tired. The anxiety from this morning, the strangeness, was creeping back into my mind. "I'm ready to go home."

"Home where? Our new home or Seven Sisters?" I didn't know if he was joking or what, but I wasn't in the mood.

"*Notre petite maison.* I just want to be with you." I sighed and closed my eyes.

"What did you say?"

"I said I want to go to Our Little Home. Not Seven Sisters."

"No, you said '*notre petite maison*'. But you don't speak French. What's that about?"

I felt the blood drain from my face. *What was going on?* I smiled awkwardly. "Maybe I heard that somewhere."

He frowned and eyed me suspiciously. "Let's go, then. I'll cook us something, and we can talk."

I nodded my head against his shoulder. "I would like that." *I have so much to tell you.* When we arrived home, thankfully the front door was neatly closed and there were no leaves on the porch and sidewalk. Doreen's car was gone, but she had left the house neat and tidy. Lightning cracked again, and this time the rain began to fall, heavy, soaking drops. I tossed my purse on the foyer table under the gilded mirror and stared at the stairs. Doreen had dutifully cleaned up the blood, and you'd never know what had happened earlier. I was glad for that and happy that Simmons hadn't taken the liberty of wrapping yellow tape across our front door. Wouldn't the neighbors have loved that?

Ashland wrapped his strong arms around me, and we kissed like we hadn't kissed since our honeymoon. He led me gently by the hand to the bottom of the stairs, but my feet wouldn't let me go up. I couldn't go up there, not right now, but I wanted him as much as he wanted me.

"No, I have a better idea." We had a barely used guest room on the other side of the kitchen. I smiled and pulled him in that direction. Ashland's sexy grin told me he liked the idea, and he followed me into the room. It felt cool and fresh—and presumably free of lurking ghosts and unhappy entities. I liked this room. We fell on the soft down comforter together and spent the next half hour lost in one another's arms. How wonderful to be with the man I loved! We needed this. I needed him! I loved him with every fiber of my being.

"I love you, Ashland Gregory Stuart." He showered my neck with kisses, and I laughed as his lips whispered across my skin.

Hoyt! Hoyt, I love you! Christine's pleading voice whispered in my head. I smothered the urge to spring up from the bed. Instead, I closed my eyes and forced myself to focus on the moment—this moment, in this lifetime. I was alive and here with my husband.

What do I do about you, Christine? What am I supposed to do? Ashland stroked my cheek with his finger and I whispered, "Hold me tight, Ashland."

"I love you, my wife. Are you hungry yet?"

"Starving! Are you sure you want to cook, though? You've had a long day already."

"I like cooking for you. And believe it or not, I couldn't find a decent meal in New Orleans."

"I do find that hard to believe!" I said with a laugh. "Okay, well, at least let me chop up some vegetables or toss a salad or something."

"That's a deal." We kissed and got dressed, and then I padded off to the restroom to work up a decent-looking ponytail. I took a ponytail holder out of the bathroom closet and checked my hair in the mirror. I didn't mind a sloppy ponytail, but my curls could look crazy if I didn't have a care for the finished product. Unhappy with the ponytail I'd made, I took it down and tried again.

Can you hear me? I know you can hear me. Please help me!

This couldn't be happening! *Go away!*

Suddenly the mirror began to reflect a smoky image. I looked behind me, but there was nothing. I stumbled back against the wicker hamper and stared at the mirror. I didn't speak, I couldn't! All I could do was gape at the outline of a woman's face struggling to appear in the smoke.

"Christine?" I gasped at the apparition.

"Hey, did you hear me?" Ashland barged into the bathroom, and I turned my attention from the mirror for a second. Even the voice had quieted in Ashland's presence. "What is it, Carrie Jo? You look like you've seen a..." His smile disappeared, and he pushed the door all the way open.

"I think I have."

"What? Here?"

I reached for his hand, and he pulled me out of the bathroom. "Okay, let's forget dinner. We'll order out— we have to talk."

"I agree. And I need a drink. How about you?"

"Yes, please." I followed him into the living room and flopped on the suede blue leather couch. I couldn't stop shaking. I wasn't necessarily afraid of Christine, but encountering ghosts or whatever that was always set my nerves on edge. It wasn't a natural thing. Not at all.

Help me.

Unleashing my wild hair from the ponytail holder, I accepted the small snifter of brandy that Ashland handed me and moved the pillow so he could sit beside me. "I don't know where to begin."

"When did all this start? Have you been dreaming about the house again?"

"That's the thing. I haven't been dreaming. In fact, until yesterday, I haven't had a dream in about three months. But I've been so happy with our new life and all, I haven't thought much about it. Then I started to experience this feeling, like something was…what's the word I'm looking for?"

"Undone?"

"Exactly. Undone. Like a wrong note played in a song you know or a whisper that you can't quite make out."

"I've felt the same thing. I thought it was just me."

I squeezed his hand, and we sipped our drinks. "Do you think we missed something?"

"Maybe. I'm not the expert, though."

"I'm sure not either," I said wryly.

"What else? Tell me what else has happened?"

"That feeling I described, it got stronger as the weeks went by. Then when you left for New Orleans, I felt like a jerk. I went downstairs to catch you before you left and found the door wide open. Not only that, but there were piles of leaves all over the place, like the door had been left open for days. That happened a few times. Including this morning, when Detra Ann got shot. And that's not all."

"Yes?"

"She's here…Isla. I've heard her giggling."

"Are you sure?"

"Well, I can't say a hundred percent, but I am pretty sure. The day you left I was working in the office when she went sailing by my door. She's back, and that can only mean one thing—we missed something."

He swirled the amber drink in his glass and downed it. "Damn," he muttered, setting the glass on the coffee table. "I wonder what it could be."

It was my turn to down my drink. "More, please." Ashland took our glasses and refilled them. A branch began to tap on the window; the storm outside had kicked up the evening breeze and the rain continued to fall.

"After that, I decided to get out of the house as quickly as I could. I drove to Bette's house, but she wasn't home. All I could think was to go to Seven Sisters. Detra Ann told me at the luncheon about the night tours, so I thought I might see Rachel and kill some time until I felt brave enough to come back here."

"You should have called me. I would have come right home, or you could have driven to New Orleans."

"Really? Because when you left I wasn't getting that vibe from you at all. It felt like you wanted to be alone, so I left you alone. For the record, I did call. You were at a party."

He laughed. "I wasn't at a party, CJ. I was at a supper club, Henri's club in New Orleans. I didn't tell you because I didn't want you to worry. I guess I was just trying to protect you."

"You saw Henri?" I couldn't help but smile. Even though he'd been caught up in Mia's web, at least at the beginning, he'd proven to be a worthy friend to

Ashland and me. He'd left Mobile after the incident in the Moonlight Garden. I didn't blame him. Not one bit.

"I did. I haven't been completely honest with you. I've been back to the house too."

"What? Why?"

"That same feeling that something was off. Detra Ann called me a few weeks ago and reminded me that I left a few crates there. I should have told you, and I'm sorry I didn't. I admit I was happy to get the call—that was my excuse to go back. Especially after all the fuss I made about deeding the house to the city. I loaded up the crates and then took a walk around the property."

"And?"

"And nothing—not at first. There were tons of visitors there, walking through the house and the gardens. It was so crowded." I could tell he was pleased about that. I was too. "Re-enactors were scattered around the property, talking to guests and pointing out some of the architectural details and the 'acceptable' history. It was exactly as we hoped. The people love it, CJ."

I smiled, happy that he was happy. Restoring Seven Sisters had been a real dream of his. "You knew they would."

"I hoped. You helped make that happen." He sipped his brandy again and continued, "I walked through the gardens toward the back of the property, where it meets the Mobile River. The grounds team that TD hired did a remarkable job of cleaning it up and bringing it back to life. I decided to walk down to the riverbank. It was a good hike, but I wanted the time to think. I felt like I was being watched, but I kept walking. I wasn't sure where I was going, but then I saw a woman peeking out from behind a tree. She wore a full-skirted gray dress with black lace trim. I thought for a minute she might be one of the re-enactors from the house, but as I got closer, I knew she wasn't."

"What did she look like?"

"Attractive, but not beautiful like Calpurnia. Sweet. She had a sweet, round face. She was about your height, maybe an inch shorter, and looked to be in her early thirties."

"Okay. What else?"

"Thinking she needed help, I shouted to her, 'Are you okay?' She stepped on to the path and faced me—she was about fifty feet away." Ashland took another sip of his drink. Anxiety crept over me—what happened next? I didn't rush him, but it took great restraint. "She raised her hand above her eyes, like you do when you're trying to block the sun. But the weird thing was, the sun was behind her. She called out, 'Hoyt! Is that you?'"

The hair on my arms began to crackle. I froze—my eyes widened at hearing someone else speak that name. "Oh, no," I whispered.

"I said, 'No, ma'am. I'm Ashland. May I help you?' Without a word, she ducked back into the woods and ran from me. I called after her, asking her if she needed help, but she didn't answer. I could hear the leaves crunching under her shoes and the swishing of her skirts, but when I made it to the point in the path where she had stood, she'd disappeared. But there was no pathway. And she couldn't have run through that section of woods, too much underbrush. No way she would have made it with those skirts. I ducked through, trying to look for any trace of her, maybe a footprint or a bit of cloth, but I didn't find anything."

Peering into the brown liquid in the glass, I asked, "Didn't you recognize her, Ashland?"

"I don't think so. It wasn't Calpurnia. I know her face. And it certainly wasn't Isla."

"No, it was neither one of them. You saw Christine, Calpurnia's mother, and she's looking for the man she loves—she's looking for Hoyt Page."

"Hoyt? Who's Hoyt?"

"He's the man she should have married. I believe he is Calpurnia's father."

"What? Who is he?"

Taking my drink with me, I walked to the back door and pushed open the curtain. The rain still streamed down, and the gutters were full of water; they poured off the side of the house. Somewhere, a cat begged to come inside. I touched the crystal glass to my lip. The scent of brandy comforted me.

Hoyt! Where are you?

For the next hour, I told Ashland everything. About the dream. About connecting with Christine. About running from Jeremiah. He didn't question me or interrupt me. It felt good to tell it, to tell it all.

"That's it. We have to find this other daughter, the one that's missing. Christine needs to know she's okay. Right? Is that what this is about?"

"I don't know. I would think so. At least, it's a place to start."

"But where do we start? Have you seen this girl?"

"I haven't...but I think Mia has. She sent me this book, that's the book I found the day you left for New Orleans. In the note, Mia says that once I read it, I will understand why she did what she did. I don't know if that's true or not, but I think there could be something significant in there."

"Well, we don't have any other clues to go on. Sounds like you, Mrs. Researcher, will be doing some research." Suddenly, Ashland laughed. It was a strange sound after everything we'd talked about. "You know, if this historian thing doesn't work out for you, you could open a detective business. Mysteries seem to follow you, Carrie Jo."

I raised my eyebrows and shook my head. "No thanks. I prefer dusty old books to voices in my head and bad dreams. Thank you, by the way, for believing me."

"Of course. If you're crazy, I'm crazy too. I've seen a few things myself, remember. I hope I never see Isla again."

"That's another thing. TD has seen her and is scared to death."

"Why would she show herself to him?"

"Why not? When she was alive, she was quite lovely. And if she thought she could use him for her own means, then…"

"That doesn't sound right. We found the treasure—why is she hanging around? Where are Calpurnia and Muncie?"

"I'm sure they are resting, Ash. Their part in this craziness is over, at least I think it is, but Christine's isn't yet. As long as there are secrets, Isla will have some measure of power."

"Great. That's just great."

"I think you're in the clear. You stood up to her. But we have to help TD. She's terrorizing him, Ashland, and he doesn't know what to do. Instead of doing this by ourselves, we have friends who will help us. We just need to come up with a plan."

"Then it's a good thing I went to see Henri."

"Why do you say that?"

"Because he's willing to help. Because he knows more than we do about all this stuff. And because, like you, I trust him."

"I think you should call him and ask him to come back to Mobile." Despite all the supernatural storytelling, I felt warm and comfortable now. Maybe it was the brandy or just being with Ashland. The rain had begun to slack now, and we cuddled up together on the couch. Neither of us was ready to break the mood.

"I will do that. You ready to go to bed?"

We'd forgotten all about eating, and I was too drowsy to think about it now. "Can't we sleep here tonight?"

His arm was behind his head, and I was lying on his chest. Sometime during our chat, I'd grabbed the chenille throw off the back of the couch and covered us with it.

"Sounds perfect," he said, kissing the top of my head. Smiling, I snuggled up to him and listened to the sound of his heart beating. I loved him so much. I couldn't believe how lucky I had been to find him. I wished Christine had had a happy ending. How many times did she lie on Hoyt's chest and listen to his heart beat?

Christine, I'm sorry for what happened to you.

I fell asleep and stepped into a dream, but it wasn't mine.

Chapter Twelve

"Calpurnia, dearest. Come show Mother what you found. Oh, look at this, Hoyt."

The little girl danced in a circle, swirling her skirts about her. The tiny ladybug on her finger refused to fly.

Screwing up her face, she stared at it. "She won't fly, Mother. Why won't she fly?"

"Maybe she needs a rest, dearest. Proper ladybugs rest in between flights."

"Is that true, Dr. Page?" With an untrusting look, the four-year-old tilted her pretty head and questioned her mother's friend.

"Yes, that is quite true."

Christine plucked at the petals of the white daisy she held. How childish to play games like "He Loves Me, He Loves Me Not." Even her soul knew that Hoyt Henry Page loved her beyond reasoning—as much as she loved him. What a picture the three of them made! Quite like a happy family enjoying a summer day by the water. But that was only a picture—an ever-fading dream buried in her heart.

Calpurnia spun around again, trying in earnest to force the bug to fly.

"Your sister came calling yesterday, Hoyt."

"Claudette? I suppose she came to bring Calpurnia a birthday gift?"

"No. In fact, she did not mention her at all."

Hoyt rose from his reclining position. He dusted the elbow of his sleeve and looked at her. He didn't dare hold her hand or touch her in public, but he had the sudden urge to do so. Christine knew this, and it assured her of his love.

"What then was her business?"

Christine tossed the now-bare flower aside and smiled at him. "She requested a meeting with Mr. Cottonwood. When I pressed her, she implied that it was business, but I know better."

"I see. What did Claudette say that would lead you to that conclusion?"

Christine raised her hand to her eyes to shield them from the sun. "Calpurnia! Come back this way. Stay away from the water!"

Frustrated, Hoyt scolded her, "Christine, you're being evasive."

"My daughter is perilously close to the river, Hoyt. Calpurnia!"

Hoyt stung at the phrase "my daughter." It was just the two of them. Couldn't Christine even then say "Our daughter?"

He brushed off her concern and tried not to appear hurt. "She will come to no harm. See? She's just spinning about. Now tell me what troubles you about my sister's visit?"

"It was a pretense, Hoyt. She has no real business with Jeremiah, none at all. She came to tell him. About us. I am sure of it."

He laughed. "She knows nothing. I have told her nothing. She has seen nothing." He tossed his hat on the blanket beside him and secretively reached for her pale hand. Such a lovely hand. Well-sculpted like a Grecian statue. "For the record, Claudette has a keen business sense. She handles all my finances."

Christine pulled her hand away in frustration. "Always willing to defend her. She knows, and she will make sure that my husband hears her out. Why has she never married? Perhaps if she were married, she would be less prone to interfere with matters that do not concern her."

"That is just her way, Christine. I promise you that I will speak to her this evening and see what is on her mind. Do not worry so."

Her heart felt instantly lighter but before she could thank him, a loud splash into the nearby water grabbed her attention. "Calpurnia!" she screamed in terror. "Ma fille!" Hoyt raced past her and in a few seconds had leaped into the water after the child. Christine stood on the riverbank, her chest heaving, anguished tears in her eyes.

Immediately she began to plead, "God, punish me but not my child! Please, not my child!" She began to pray to the Virgin as Hoyt swam to Callie, whose sweet face was immersed in the troubled waters of the river.

"Calpurnia! Calpurnia!" Finally Hoyt reached her and turned her upright. The child did not move but floated like a dead leaf on the water. "Calpurnia!" Hoyt struggled against the current but finally reached the muddy shore. Exhausted, he lifted the child out of the water and collapsed on the bank. Christine ran to them, crying and pleading with God to save her daughter.

She peeled long strands of wet hair off the child's face and gasped. Calpurnia's lips were blue, her skin cold and clammy. "She is dead. Oh mon ame! Come back to me, my child!"

Hoyt shook off the weariness and lifted the child up to his shoulder. He patted her back, attempting to force the water from her lungs. He wept as he smacked her tiny back until finally, he heard her wheeze.

"Hoyt!" Christine's face appeared unbelieving for a second, then a smile flashed across it. "She's moving! She is alive! Grace a Dieu!"

"Let's get the child home. She needs some attention. Get the carriage, Christine."

"Yes, of course." She ran back to the lane and appeared in a few minutes with Hoyt's open carriage. Calpurnia had not roused, but she was breathing. She was alive—and that was all that mattered to Christine. They did not talk as they raced back to Seven Sisters. Christine held her water-logged child to her chest and kissed her head repeatedly. "You will be alright, cherie. See? We are almost home, dearest." The child could not open her eyes, but her tiny chest rose and fell. Christine watched each breath with worry. They raced down the red clay lane that led to Seven Sisters. In seconds, tall, gangly Stokes ran out to meet them. Christine handed him the child and said, "Take her to her room."

"Yes, ma'am. Mr. Cottonwood is looking for you in his study." He did not look Christine in the eye but took the damp bundle she presented him.

"I will see him. Take her upstairs to her room and give Dr. Page whatever he needs. I'll come as soon as I can." She searched his face for a clue about her husband's request, but there were none forthcoming. Stokes had been and always would be the master's most dependable slave, faithful above all others.

"Yes, ma'am."

Now that the immediate emergency had been handled, Christine could breathe again. Hoyt would see to it that their daughter would recover. She knew it. Her gown was wet and muddy, and she imagined that her hair was messy, but there was nothing she could do about that now. Jeremiah insisted that she appear like a lady at all times, but surely such an emergency as this warranted a measure of latitude. She went in the house, down the hallway to Jeremiah's study. Nobody came to greet her or attend to her, a sure sign that something was amiss. Jeremiah stood at the window, an unlit cigar in his mouth. He wore no coat; Christine spotted his blue jacket resting on the arm of his chair. Immediately she began to worry. He wouldn't harm her with Hoyt in the house—surely not with Hoyt there. How different he looked from the man she had first met. He had been so accommodating, so eager to please her during their courtship. Christine had never had any illusions that he loved her, or she him, but she would have never dreamed that she would be so unhappy—and he so cruel.

"You wanted to see me, Jeremiah?"

He did not look at her at first, and when he did, he showed no surprise at her appearance. He barely looked in her direction. She might as well have been one of the slaves.

"I would ask you to sit, but your gown would stain my chair, I am afraid." He set the cigar in the massive crystal ashtray that rested on the edge of his desk. "You cannot know how unhappy I am, Christine. I have had a letter from your father today."

"Mon pere?"

"Yes, and please refrain from speaking French. It will do you no good. I am immune to your feminine wiles."

"Wiles?" Christine felt her pulse race. She reminded herself to remain calm. "What do you mean? I have no wiles."

Jeremiah leered at her. He strode to his desk and picked up the letter. "He says, and I quote, 'Make my good daughter aware of my correspondence, and please relay to her my fondness and pride in her situation.'"

She did not know how to respond, still unsure what crime he imagined she had committed. Her inner voice urged her again to remain calm. "I shall go write to him immediately and thank him for his kind words. Thank you for sharing them with me." She turned to leave, holding her breath for luck as she did. In just four steps he was behind her.

Grasping her arm savagely, he pulled her to him. His breath smelled stale, a sickening combination of whiskey and salted pork. "Do not walk away from me, wife! Never walk away from me. Do you understand?"

Her silver earbobs jingled as she nodded. She didn't pull away, for that would only enrage him further. She had to keep quiet until she could discern the source of his rage. Christine prayed that Claudette Page had not been successful in her desire to educate him, to fill his ears with the one thing that could destroy Christine completely. He would kill her—that much she was sure of.

"Why is he coming here? Why, Christine?"

"Who? Dr. Page? Calpurnia fell into the river, and he happened to be passing by and gave assistance. If it weren't for Dr. Page, our daughter would be..." The words began to pour out of her mouth. She detested lying. She never mastered "mensonge discrete," discreet lying as some called it. But for Hoyt, for Calpurnia, she would lie to the holy angels themselves.

"Don't play coy with me! I am speaking of your brother!" He shoved the letter at her and commanded her to read it. Fearful of what he might do next, she hastily began to read. "Esteemed Son-In-Law..."'

"Damnation! Skip down to the last paragraph. Read it! Convince me that you did not call him here!"

"'In the interest of our mutual benefit and kind relationship, please receive my son Louis with all courtesy when he arrives at the end of this month. I have entrusted him to carry out my business and have requested his assistance in procuring the adjoining lands to the south of Seven Sisters. He has also requested a review of the most recent financial records, and I trust you will accommodate him in this matter.'"

"Louis is coming here? I swear, mon mari—I mean, my husband—I did not know! I have not written him or my father since this spring. He has not come at my request."

He stomped toward Christine and snatched the letter from her, reading it silently to himself. Fighting every instinct in her soul, mind and body, she stood rigidly, almost defiantly. In this she was innocent!

"You think I believe you? I know you swoon and pant after Louis Beaumont. He is the only man you have ever truly loved, isn't he, Christine." He stomped back to his desk and sat in the heavy wooden chair.

"He is my brother, Jeremiah! How dare you suggest such a thing?!"

"Don't play the frightened damsel with me, wife."

She could bear the insults. It was nothing in comparison to the truth, was it? "I swear to you, Jeremiah, on everything I treasure, I did not write to Louis. Whatever he and my father have planned, I know nothing."

"So you say. How can I trust you?" He poured himself another glass of whiskey, tossed it back and closed his eyes. Christine breathed a quiet sigh of relief. He didn't know! He knew nothing about Hoyt! Not yet. Bravely, she continued to stand before him. Eventually he looked up, his eyes bleary and red. "Go, and for God's sake, do something with yourself. No more gardening today, Christine."

With a curt nod, she left the room, closing the doors behind her. As quickly as she could, she ran up the stairs to her daughter and Hoyt. Her heart skipped a beat when she heard her daughter crying loudly.

Just a little longer together, Hoyt! We have just a little longer!

I'm coming, Calpurnia! Mother is coming!

Chapter Thirteen

"Momma?" My eyes felt heavy, and my entire body hurt like I'd been hit by a Mack truck, especially my left side. Confusion and pain collided, and I caught my breath.

"Detra Ann! You're awake! Nurse! She's…" The words sounded muffled and I strained to hear but fell asleep again. Suddenly a beam of light hit my left eye, and I felt my eyes flutter open.

"Momma? Where am I?"

I began to see clearly now. Sunlight peeked through cheap plastic blinds, and the walls were a horrid mauve with grey plastic trim. Medical machines were beeping around me. My mother hovered over me, her pearls dangling from her neck and ears; she was wearing her yellow suit, the one with the tiny yellow flowers at the lapel. She always wanted to look like she'd stepped out of the Sears and Roebuck catalog, she said. How sad that they don't send out those catalogs anymore. Still, my mother could be kind, if a bit overprotective.

"Are you awake again? Detra Ann?"

"Yes, I'm awake."

"You are at the hospital," she said slowly and loudly like I was hearing-impaired.

I tried to sit up, but a sharp, stabbing pain tore through my side.

"Don't move, alright? The doctor is on…his…way."

"I'm not deaf, Momma. Please, can you get me a glass of water?"

"I don't think you're supposed to drink anything yet. Not this soon after surgery."

"Surgery? Please get me some water."

"Detra Ann? You're awake." TD hovered over me now. I ignored Mother's pursed lips and the eye roll that seemed to accompany all her conversations or interactions with him. He kissed my hand—he was as handsome as ever. His hair was slightly longer and messier than I last remembered...I kind of liked it. I touched it as he leaned forward. No matter how lost he was, TD always smelled like sawdust and sunshine.

"Hey, baby. Does this mean we're back together?" Oh Lord! I was never this needy—what was I saying?

"I'm here, Detra Ann, and your mother is too."

I whispered through dry lips, "I need something to drink."

"Be right back."

As he disappeared from my view, I struggled to get my bearings. The pain in my side was excruciating—I had nothing to compare it to. I'd never had children or any major surgery, except for that time I broke my finger on the playground. That had been Ashland's fault, but I never told anyone. He hadn't meant to smash my finger with that teeter-totter. Oh, and I'd had my wisdom teeth removed too. How sick I had been that night.

Something about the pain medicine made me sick. Oh my God! The pain was unbearable.

"Listen, dear, the doctor has you on a drip—see the tube? The button is right here. When you start hurting, press the button. You will recover, but it is going to hurt for a while. Don't be a hero, Detra Ann."

"I won't," I said glumly, immediately pressing the button.

"What happened? Why were you in that woman's house?"

"Somebody pushed me, I think." I remembered climbing up the stairs, calling for Carrie Jo... "Carrie Jo...is she okay? Did they hurt her too?"

TD returned with a cup, and I prayed it was water. I could see the IV bag pumping fluids into my body, but I was so thirsty.

"The nurse says you can't drink any water but you can have ice chips, if that makes any sense. Here you go, baby."

I took the cup in my hands as Momma slowly eased my bed up a few inches. "That's good. It hurts too bad to move up any higher. Thanks for the ice." The pain medicine was working again—I felt no pain at all now. I scooped up a few ice chips in my mouth and crunched them. They were the best things I had ever put in my mouth. "Somebody hit me in the stomach and I fell down the stairs. I couldn't see who it was, but it wasn't Carrie Jo. She was in the hallway. Wait, I do remember someone being on the stair with me. What was her name? Why can't I think?" My brain felt like it was wrapped in damp cotton.

"It's the pain medicine," my mother whispered to TD.

"Wait, she's not supposed to be there. She lives at Seven Sisters, right? I wonder why she was at Carrie Jo's house."

"Who, baby?" My mother patted my forehead with a damp cloth.

"Isla. Yeah, that's it."

TD's face turned deathly pale. He said, "What did you say, babe? Isla?"

"Yes, she pushed me down the stairs at CJ's house. Oh, TD! It was the scariest thing I ever saw. She was right in front of me—she just popped up out of nowhere. I found the front door open, and I got worried for Carrie Jo. She'd had a bad night at the house, we both did. Jeremiah Cottonwood tried to get us, but we ran and ran…"

"What are you talking about?" My mother's face reflected her shock. "Is she talking about *the* Jeremiah Cottonwood? Is that who you mean? He is dead, Detra Ann, and has been dead for over a hundred years."

"Cynthia, I think it's the meds talking. Don't take anything she says seriously," TD lied to my mother. He knew that what was happening at Seven Sisters was real—very real.

"How can you say that, TD? I saw her. I know I did." I summoned up her face from my fragmented memory.

She had appeared just inches in front of my face. I wasn't sure how I knew her name or how she knew mine, but she did.

Go home, Detra Ann! Her face twisted into a snarl, the voice in my head full of inhuman viciousness. I remembered that she'd startled me and then struck me hard in the gut. "I'm so tired."

"Rest now. I'll be here when you wake up," TD whispered in my ear. "I love you."

"I love you too," I said, at least in my mind.

Then I wasn't in the hospital room anymore.

I found myself standing in the ballroom of Seven Sisters. Shadowy couples dressed in black swirled about me, dancing to a macabre waltz played by an invisible orchestra. The massive chandelier above me shone with amber light that cast living shadows on the walls of the room. The black-clad dancers did not seem to notice me, but I could feel the silk rubbing against my skin as they moved around and around. With escalating alarm, I pushed my way through the couples; their indiscernible faces did not acknowledge me, but somehow I knew they were aware of my presence—and I was an unwanted guest. I didn't belong here. My side hurt and my skin grew cold, the thin hospital gown providing me little comfort. I stumbled forward, terror rising inside me. What if I could not get out?

"Please," I shouted, "please let me out!" I reached out to touch the shoulder of a man who swung by me in a perfect circle. He robotically turned his face to me, but none of his features were clear except his hate-filled eyes.

"Where is your invitation?" he demanded as he and his partner swooped around me.

Sobbing now, I pushed on. My side burned, and I imagined that I felt blood dripping from the wound. Time had no meaning here in this ballroom of specters, but I knew I had walked much further than was necessary to reach that door. Again silk slapped my face and bodies pushed against me as I shoved my way to the exit.

"Let me go! Let me out!"

My cries went unheard over the noise of the scratchy violins. Finally, in the briefest of moments, the couples in front of me moved and I could plainly see the door. I was almost there! Again they shoved against me. Weeping and reaching, I said, "You have no right to keep me here!"

Then the chandelier dimmed as I made a final push to escape the spinning crowd. I extended my shaking hand toward the door with every ounce of energy I had. Somehow I knew this was my last push, my last try. If I wasn't successful now, if I couldn't break free, I would be here forever. I felt the tears welling up in my eyes.

Then she appeared—Isla! Hovering between me and the door. With a kittenish smile and fierce eyes, she floated closer. I had nowhere to go. The dancers whirled behind me in their evil circles—the only way out was before me.

"No, Christine. You can't leave yet. You haven't been properly received, and he's waiting for you. He's been waiting, and now the wait is over. Take my hand, Christine, and it will all be over." She reached her hand out to me, only a few feet away. I stared at it. It was a lifeless, pale thing, so small and childlike. So young, so perfect.

So dead.

I opened my mouth to protest, but all that came out was a scream.

Chapter Fourteen

I woke up to the smells of breakfast and the sound of Ashland calling my name. I stretched like a lazy cat and followed my nose to the kitchen. My husband had taken a shower, set the bar for breakfast and had everything ready for me before I got up. "Morning," he said, "How did you sleep?"

"Great. How is your shoulder? I hope I didn't drool on you."

He laughed. "No but you do talk in your sleep."

Sitting at the bar, I slid my plate his way to accept a few spoonfuls of scrambled eggs. "Did I at least say anything interesting?"

"I'll never tell," he teased.

I sipped the hot coffee and wolfed down my bacon and eggs. It felt like forever since I'd eaten. I had managed to grab some chips from the vending machine at the hospital but had never opened them. "Boy, that was delicious. Anything else in there?"

"Check the fridge. I think there is some fruit salad if you want that."

"Yuck, I'll pass. I better get a shower before we head to Springhill. I assume we're going first thing?"

"I'd like to. I'll tidy up here."

Hopping out of the chair, I kissed his cheek and took my coffee cup with me. "Give me ten minutes."

"You got it."

During my walk up the stairs, I focused on not spilling my coffee, not on the spot where Detra Ann fell or on the tiny hole in the wall from the bullet. I hoped she was going to be all right. As quickly as I could, I rummaged for some casual yet presentable clothing and then headed to the shower. I didn't look in any mirrors or even glance around the room. If there was something here, I didn't want to know. Drinking down the last swigs of my coffee, I took my shower and got dressed in record time. No sense in dawdling and giving Isla a chance to reappear. I stopped for a moment. Nope, nothing. Hmm…things were oddly quiet this morning.

Ashland rapped on the door. "Almost done," I called.

"We have to go. Something's happened to Detra Ann!"

"What?" I flung the door open as I buttoned up my pants. "What happened?"

"I don't know. TD said something about a seizure— now she's in a coma. I don't know. Are you ready?"

"Yes, let me grab my shoes and purse."

"I'll be in the car."

"Okay, be there in a sec!" I towel-dried my hair and grabbed a hair clip. *Not fooling with my hair today.* Two minutes later I ran after him, grabbing my purse off the foyer table as I practically ran out the door. Locking it behind me, I yelled up the stairwell, "You're not going to win, Isla!" I don't know why I did it, but it felt good.

I was angry, angrier than I had been in a long time. I didn't hear a sound, not even a giggle.

As Ashland navigated the busy streets, I sent TD a few texts to let him know we were close, but he didn't answer. "Must be with Detra Ann," I told Ashland. "God, I hope she's okay."

"Me too. She's like a sister to me, you know. She is the nearest thing to family that I have. Besides you, of course." His voice shook as he turned into the parking lot.

I didn't know what to say. I rubbed his shoulder as we whizzed down Springhill Avenue. A few minutes later, we pulled into an open spot. It was a good thing we'd gotten here early, as the parking lot was nearly full. A few minutes later we were stepping off the elevator onto the fifth floor of the hospital. When the doors opened Ashland and I both froze—the place was full of women from the Historical Society. A nurse approached our group and asked us to relocate to the waiting room. We complied, but some of the society did not go without some mild protests.

"Ashland! Carrie Jo!" People hugged me like they'd known me all my life. "So sad what's happened! How in the world did she get shot? Now she's in a coma!"

My plan was to let Ashland field these questions. I'd stay in the background until I could see Detra Ann. But Holliday Betbeze had other plans. She found an empty seat beside me and attempted to probe me for more information.

"Were you robbed? Is that what happened? Did Detra Ann protect you from a thief? You know, that is a very dangerous part of town. My own cousin was robbed down there just two streets over."

"I didn't know that," I said, attempting to deflect her questioning.

"Tell me the truth, why on earth did you and Ashland ever give up that big old house? I would have stayed there until they drug me out by my shoelaces."

"You know you don't own a pair of shoelaces, Holliday," another woman chimed in. For a few minutes, they forgot about me and chatted about the tragedy and the "Seven Sisters" curse. After a while, Cynthia came out of her daughter's room and soon became the group's new center of gravity. Ashland hugged her and said something in her ear. She nodded and smiled weakly before patting him gently on the shoulder. After a few seconds, he walked out of the room, leaving me behind without a word. I gave Cynthia a polite smile and tried to follow after him as quickly as I could. It didn't happen.

"Wait, Carrie Jo." Cynthia stepped in front of me. The crowd stopped their chattering, waiting to see what happened next. In a quiet voice she said, "I want to apologize to you. I said some very rude things yesterday, and I regret them. Detra Ann told me that it wasn't your fault—and she told me what she thinks happened. And that lady detective called me to say you aren't a suspect. I was wrong. I jumped to the wrong conclusion, and I am truly sorry for that." Cynthia didn't wait for my response. She scooped me up in her thin arms and hugged me.

I squeezed her shoulders and whispered, "Don't worry about me. We're here if you need us."

She wiped at her eyes with a crumpled tissue. "Is there anything you can tell me? Anything at all? My daughter mentioned that someone else was there. Isla, I think her name was. Is she a friend of yours?"

How should I answer this? "The only person I saw was Detra Ann. I swear to you, I didn't see anyone else."

She touched my arm and nodded. "It must have been the pain medication. She's never been able to tolerate it." She walked away slowly, and I went down the hall in the direction Ashland had gone. I pushed the door open to Detra Ann's room. TD sat in the chair next to her, his long hair tucked behind his ears, his eyes bloodshot and tired-looking. Ashland stood on the other side of the bed staring down at her. Detra Ann's blond hair was spread around her like a golden halo. Her face was serene; she reminded me of Sleeping Beauty. Even though she was the picture of peace, the air around her was not.

Bette popped in the room, and she practically ran into me. "How have you been, Bette? I came by to see you, but you weren't there. Are you okay?"

With tears in her eyes, Bette nodded. I could see that she was a big old mix of emotions right now, but I had no idea why. I had not gotten the idea that she and Detra Ann were all that close. Maybe they were after all. People deal with situations like this differently.

For about the sixth time today I received an unexpected hug. But this wasn't just an "I'm here for you" hug. Bette was heartbroken. "Bette, please. You're scaring me. What has happened? Is it your son? Your boyfriend?"

She looked from me to Ashland, her heart on her sleeve. Her perfect white curls bounced as she shook her head. "Now isn't the right time to share my news. As soon as Detra Ann is better, I will tell you everything. Right now, I just wanted to see you. And I know this may sound strange, Carrie Jo, but I wanted you to know that I love you. And you too, Ashland. I love you both. No matter what happens. Now I have to go help Cynthia. I'm going to make sure she eats, even if it is in the lousy hospital cafeteria. We'll talk soon." With that, she walked out. Ashland's eyes met mine—he looked as confused as I did. What was going on with Bette?

"Ashland, we have to do something." TD sounded desperate. "What can we do? I've been here with Detra Ann, praying for her. Can you believe that? Me, praying? I won't quit, but there has to be something else. I have to do something."

I nodded and said, "I agree. Of all the people in the world, this shouldn't be happening to Detra Ann. She didn't do anything to deserve this. I think we all know that this wasn't an accident. Isla did this, and I can't understand why. I thought her power was broken, but I guess she never left."

"I can't stand sitting back and waiting. I hate playing defense." TD's deep voice shook with a mixture of anger and grief. I could tell he was considering having a drink—or five. I touched his shoulder to remind him that he wasn't alone.

Ashland shook his head. "No, we won't sit back and wait for the other shoe to drop. I'm making the call. Henri needs to be here, and whatever he tells us, we're going to do, right? Everyone agree?"

"I don't know what else we can do," I said.

"If it helps Detra Ann, of course. I'm in." He reached out, took her hand and kissed it.

"I'll go make the call." With a resolute look, Ashland left the room. That was my Ashland, always ready to rescue someone. I sighed, hoping that he was right— that Henri knew more than we did.

I sat next to TD and quietly prayed for Detra Ann. Soon, the room felt and even looked lighter. The bells on her machine rang less and her heart rate was calm.

I knew it. We weren't alone. And maybe this time, we'd get it right.

Chapter Fifteen

An hour later, it was quiet, which was a relief. The ladies had left, deciding to each cook a dish for Cynthia Dowd. It was like a wake lunch, only Detra Ann wasn't dead. It was morbid, if you asked me, but I guessed they did things differently down here in Mobile. Just one of the social quirks that made this place so unique.

I settled on a corner couch in one of the many waiting rooms in Springhill Memorial. I had a water bottle, a bag of dried pineapple from the vending machine and the book that Mia had sent me. Ashland and TD were counting on me to get to the bottom of the problem—find out why Mia and Isla felt they still had a claim on Seven Sisters. When I knew what it was, we could come up with a plan. We needed a plan, big time! I'd deliberately left the ICU floor, at Ashland's urging, in favor of the fourth-floor waiting room. There were more people here but they didn't know me or try to chat with me. I needed quiet to read, but I didn't want to go home. Not without Ashland, and he understandably wasn't leaving until Detra Ann was better.

He'd gone home and grabbed me some snacks, a toothbrush, a pillow and my favorite chenille blanket. I hated the idea of dreaming here in the hospital, but I thought I'd gotten better at controlling who I dreamed about. I'd gotten quite good at calling out names and entering the right dreams. But I was the first to admit that I had a lot to learn about dream catching.

I hunkered down on the couch, which was remarkably comfortable given the circumstances. Kicking off my shoes, I examined the book again. It felt old, small and certainly not magical. It was a plain brown leather book, but hopefully there were some words inside that were going to set us all free. Especially Detra Ann.

I skimmed through the part I'd already read. I flipped through the section about Delilah's time in Canada. Surely, whatever I needed to know about her had to do with her time in Mobile, after the war. No sense in wondering. It was time to find out.

For five years Canada was home even though it didn't feel like it. I missed Mobile, but we were surrounded by people who loved us. The Iverson clan was a hearty lot with plenty of children to keep me entertained during those long, tedious winter months locked inside away from the cold Canadian wilderness. During our stay, I had picked up a bit of our mother tongue and developed a propensity for storytelling, which according to my mother was a family tradition. I got quite good at telling stories and even began to write my own stories and plays.

Uncle Lars and his wife Aida treated me well, but their daughters were far from friendly and liked to refer to me as the "dark bird." I assumed they were referring to my dark hair and eyes, which were so markedly different from their own blond hair and blue eyes. Still, the small children liked me, and many of my male cousins treated me affectionately.

In fact, some of my cousins were so friendly that Adam came to me one afternoon and instructed me to behave less warmly with them. I admit that at the time, I was quite naïve about such things and didn't know why he was making such a fuss. It wasn't until one of my cousins proposed to me that I understood Adam warning. Marriage to a beloved cousin was an honorable thing to my family, and indeed to many people at that time, even though such an idea seems repugnant in today's world. I had no mind to marry anyone at that time, even though I am sure my parents would have found such a match pleasing and acceptable. A year after our escape from Mobile, my mother died rather quickly. Right until the end she worked in the Iversons' store alongside her sister-in-law until the morning we found her dead in her bed. Poor gentle Mother—she had been the sun in our sky, the warm embrace that held us all together.

Adam and I grieved like orphans even though our father was still very much alive. After our relocation, he spent much of his time on the trade routes with his brothers and didn't know about Mother's demise for several months. I had set pen to paper many times, but where would I send a letter? What would I say? After the trading season ended, he returned home to discover her long gone and buried. We found him there at her grave one afternoon, unable to speak or move his left arm and leg. Eating became impossible, and soon he shrank into a husk of the strapping man we knew. He followed Mother into heaven just a month after his return home. And then we were orphans in the truest since of the word.

One would think that such a tragedy, the loss of parents, would drive two siblings closer, but it did not. Adam became sullen, often angry at the mere sight of me. In turn, I did my best to avoid him, spending as much time as I could with my aunt and her many grandchildren. His moods were unpredictable—at times he would leave me bouquets of purple flowers on the sideboard. Other times, he would pore over his newspapers, reading news of the war, and would slam the door in my face if I approached his room. Soon he took to leaving me alone for days on end. I went to him once, begging him to speak to me, but he refused—until one spring evening. He'd been drinking from the brown jug that Father had kept in his desk drawer. I thought that odd because Adam never drank and showed little regard for those who did.

I had retreated to my room, shed my day dress and brushed my hair before braiding it to make ready for bed. It had been a long day. Adam had sold our parents' cabin on the outskirts of town, and we had moved into the rooms above the store as a way to save money. Adam had steady work, with many orders for new tables and chairs coming in all the time, but we had no need for a home with three bedrooms.

"Delilah!" I heard him call me. I didn't go right away, for I dreaded the idea of squabbling with the brother I loved so much. "Delilah, please come see me." Unable to resist his gentler tone, I walked into the other room, waiting to hear what he had to say. I sat in a chair near the hearth. It was chilly in my nightdress, and spring had yet to yield warmer temperatures. Adam's blond hair shone bright in the candlelight, his cheeks were pink from working outdoors.

"I think we should go home."

"We cannot go back. You sold our home, remember?"

"No." He shoved a cork in the jug and set it back in its place in Father's desk drawer. "I mean home to Mobile."

"What? This is our home now, Adam. We have no one to go back for. How can you suggest that we leave our parents?"

"Our parents are dead, Delilah. We have property in Alabama, did you know that? We retain ownership of the carpentry shop and the store—even though they are empty. I had an inquiry from a woman, a Miss Page, who wants to buy them, but I can't part with them. We could do it—we could make something for ourselves."

"What are you saying, Adam? Is the war over?"

"Yes, and Mobile is rebuilding. We should be there to help. I know you miss it! You often talk about it, the warm creeks, the hummingbirds, the blackberries."

"We aren't children anymore, Adam. We have a life here. How can we leave Uncle Lars and Aunt Aida now? After all they have done for us?"

"We have worked and earned what we have. Father left us very wealthy, Lila." He moved his chair closer to me. *"Please, come with me."*

"You sound as if you've made up your mind already. After weeks of not talking to me, of treating me like a stranger, you have the nerve to ask me to leave with you? What will you do, leave me in the wilderness somewhere?" Tears stung my eyes. How could I leave my parents behind? How could he ask me this? I would never be able to pull the weeds from their graves or visit them whenever I needed to talk.

"I love you, Delilah. With all my heart I love you." His blue eyes were full of pain, and I suddenly felt sorry for him. I squeezed his hand and kissed his cheek. How could I stay mad at my own brother? He was all the family I had now.

"I love you too, Adam. Tell me, what has been the matter? Why have you been so distant? Is it because of the war? You blame me, don't you?"

"It's not that. I can't talk about it. Please don't ask me to explain—I will one day, I promise."

That would have to do for now. Adam was an Iverson, stubborn through and through. Pressing him would only lead to more bickering. *"If I agree to this, how soon would we leave?"*

He smiled his beautiful smile as if he'd already won the argument. "It would take us a few weeks to settle our affairs here and to find passage south, and I would have to find a solicitor for our legal needs. Probably by the end of May, I would think."

"I haven't said yes yet. Let me sleep on it so that I may keep at least a shred of dignity." He hugged me, holding me close to him. I welcomed his embrace; it had been too long since we had been kind to one another. Suddenly, Adam kissed me tenderly on the neck and then released me. He walked out the door, and I watched him leave. He had never kissed me before, much less in such a personal way, and I hardly knew what to think of it. I still remember that night. How I tossed and turned, how I dwelt upon that kiss.

The next morning, I rose early to prepare his breakfast. I tried not to see the eager look on his face, but I could see he wasn't going to allow me to avoid giving my answer. "Although I am loath to leave our family, I am willing to return to Mobile if you like, at least to settle our affairs there. I want you to promise me that if I choose to return, you will not stop me."

"Why should you return here? Has anyone asked for your hand?"

"No, of course not."

He smiled again and said, "Agreed. I shall tell Uncle Lars this morning after breakfast."

"Adam, if I had said no, would you have left anyway?" What prompted me to ask such a question, I do not know, but I did want to know his answer.

He poured a cup of dark coffee and stared at me. "Does it matter now? To Mobile and to our future!" He raised his cup to me and drank from it cheerfully. He chattered about details that did not concern me. Soon he left to see our uncle. Usually I would dress and go downstairs to help in the store. Sometimes my aunt needed help moving things, and I had a knack for selling. None of her daughters came to the shop except Elsa, the oldest. Her swollen belly kept her from helping now—her new baby would arrive very soon. That morning, I dawdled amongst our things, mentally making a list of what I would keep, what I would give to my aunt and what I truly didn't need.

Walking over to the rolltop desk, I rolled back the lid. My father had built the desk when he was a boy, and it still rolled smoothly. This I would take with me. I sat down on the cushioned chair and stared at the neatly stacked letters. Taking one in my hand, I ran my finger over the script, missing him more than I had in months. I didn't cry, but my heart broke to read his letters even though they were all business transactions. I read them all, and when I was through, I opened other drawers and found other stacks of letters. Again, many of these were business-related, but finally I found one that was not.

It was a worn envelope addressed to me. I had never seen it, nor had anyone ever read it to me.

Dear Delilah,

I call you this because I hear that is what your family calls you. My name is Dr. Hoyt Page. I am a physician living in Mobile, Alabama, and I am writing to inform you that you are my daughter. Forgive me for my bluntness, but as I am ill and not likely to live through the night, I feel a sense of urgency to reach out to my only living child.

As I have stated, I am your father. Your mother was Christine Beaumont Cottonwood…"

I couldn't believe what I was reading! Delilah was the baby! I immediately sent Ashland a text.

Big news in book! I'm going to keep reading, but I will come up and see you in about an hour. You still there??

A few seconds later he responded: *Yes, Detra Ann is stable now but still unconscious. I will be here.*

I scanned the waiting room. I could hardly believe this bombshell I was reading. Nobody paid me a bit of attention, which was great. I tucked in my headphones, tapped on an instrumental song on my phone and continued to read. I couldn't stop now!

Your mother was Christine Beaumont Cottonwood, and she died the night you were born. There is no way, my dear, to pretty up the facts. Christine was a married woman, married to a horrible man, Jeremiah Cottonwood, whom I recently killed. It was quite easy to do, as I have hated him for such a long time. I set upon him as he was riding drunk on his way home again to Seven Sisters. I stepped out of the shadows and shot him dead. Now he had paid for his crimes against your dear mother. The man was a monster and deserved his fate. I have avenged your mother's death, and soon I will join her. Please do not think too meanly of me to have done this deed—how could I allow him to go on living? In the case of your mother, justice moved too slowly for us all.

What else should I say to you except that I am sorry, truly sorry, for the misfortune that fate seems to have dealt you? You are the daughter of a Beaumont. That may not seem like much at the moment, but it is a special thing. You are also my daughter, the child of a prosperous doctor, and I have left everything I own to you. Won't my sister be surprised to learn about you! Your aunt, Claudette, is not a woman to be crossed, so be kind to her.

Perhaps you can give her one of the houses I have bequeathed to you.

I wish we had had a different life, Christine and I, but it wasn't to be. We had our moment in the sun, and you are our proof that our love was real. You had a sister, Calpurnia, but she has been missing for nearly seventeen years. I cannot prove this, but I feel sure that Mr. Cottonwood killed her after your own dear mother died, knowing that Christine would have left your sister the heir to her fortune. I hope that somehow you will forgive me, forgive us, for not being the kind of people who could care for someone as special and lovely as you.

I imagine you often. I wonder if you like singing and playing music as Christine did, or maybe you prefer drawing, reading and writing as did your sister. I wish you were here so I could steal a look at you, as I did so many times when you were a child.

Please know that if I had believed the Iversons to be unsuitable people to serve as parents for my daughter, I would have taken you from them without a word or thought. But even I, a man who has never had a wife and family to call his own, could see that you were happy. I saw you many times, working in the shop and sometimes in attendance at church. I had hoped one day that you would return to Mobile to see me or that perhaps, once the war was over, I might go to see you, but such a visit is impossible now.

I love you more than I love my last breath. I love you more than I love even my own sister. I pray that you have a happy life. Think of me not as a vulgar man but as a fallible one who loved your mother and my children the best way I knew how.

Yours truly,

Your father,

Dr. Henry Hoyt Page

Can you imagine, Ernesto, what I felt as I read that letter? Knowing the truth forever changed me! I imagine some might feel betrayed to know that her parents were not her blood kin. Some women might feel angry at being pushed to the side so that her parents could continue their illicit affair undisturbed. Others might begrudge the inevitable title of "bastard," but I felt no shame about it.

No! I was free, Ernesto! Free like the Great Wind that blew through Shakespeare's plays. Free like a young colt that's discovered there is life outside the prison of the corral! Everything made sense now! I clutched the letter to my heart and spun about the room. I did not know this man who claimed to be my father; indeed, I did not even know if his words were true. I did know that now, more than anything else, I wanted to go to Mobile. I had to go and see what my true father had left me. I wanted to know about him and my mother. I would always love my Iverson family, but I was old enough now to know the truth about who I was! I truly was the "dark bird!" A bird of another flock!

But what about Adam? What did this mean for him? Was it my property he was thinking of claiming for himself? I tucked the letter in my dress pocket and continued to search. In the hidden compartment under the desk I found three more letters. One was from the Miss Page that Adam had spoken about. With shaking fingers I opened the letter and read it feverishly.

…wish to purchase the sundries store on Royal Street. Please let me know…

Thank God! How would I feel knowing that my own brother would be willing to steal from me, his sister? Wait! I was not his sister. We were raised as such, but there was not an ounce of Iverson blood in my body. And Adam, well, he was a Norwegian through and through. Suddenly, I heard him bounding up the

*stairs. He must have received a happy answer from our—his—
uncle. He came into the room with a smile on his face, but it
quickly faded as he saw the letter in my hand and the state of the
desk.*

*"Adam," I whispered, unsure of what I wanted to say. He didn't
ask any questions; he tossed his hat on the table and closed the
door behind him. I walked toward him, Miss Page's letter in my
hands. All of a sudden I knew the truth, the mind-blowing truth:
I loved him. I loved him like a woman loves a man. By the kiss
he had given me earlier, I knew he felt the same way. He knew
the truth and had probably known for some time but had kept it
from me.*

*I didn't know what I should say, so I said nothing at first. Then,
with a trembling voice I said, "I know who I am now. I know
that I am not your sister."*

*He nodded, looking relieved, his fair complexion an embarrassed
pink. At last, the weight of the truth lifted off of him, but he
didn't move. I knew that he would never care that some might call
me bastard. He didn't care what anyone thought, and neither did
I. For the first time, I kissed him. Chastely at first and then
passionately. It sounds strange, doesn't it, Ernesto? That I could
so freely kiss a man whom I had previously considered my brother.
It sounds strange and unholy to me even now, but I think we
always knew.*

*We did not kiss again after that, not for many weeks. We spent
our time packing and preparing for our trip. I asked him one
quiet evening while we sat in the nearly empty house how long he
had known the truth. He confessed that he had always known,
that he remembered the day I came to live with his family, a frail
child who cried constantly. But it wasn't until recently that he
realized he loved me. He had promised our mother that he would*

never tell me, but my discovery of the letter had freed him from that constraint.

Adam advised me to refrain from telling the Iversons about our relationship, for they would not approve. In the Old World, adopted children are considered blood kin. So we kept our secret and left with their blessing. I genuinely felt heartsick about leaving my aunt and her grandchildren.

I won't bore you, Ernesto, with the details of our trip. The days were long and tedious with too much riding and not enough walking. Adam treated me well, making sure that I was as comfortable as possible in whatever carriage, train or wagon we found ourselves in. However, he was still changeable. At times, he introduced me as his sister, at other times as his fiancée, although he had not actually proposed. It did not escape my notice that these "sister" introductions were typically made in the presence of other young women, women that Adam might have had an eye for.

Truth be told, I spent half the journey to the Gulf Coast not speaking to him. For two months we traveled and never did he kiss me again.

We arrived in Mobile on a Tuesday. The dirt streets in front of our shops were muddy, but from the wagon we could see that somehow the businesses had made it through the war without any missing walls or fallen roofs. "See! That's a sign!" Adam said excitedly. We looked for lodgings for the next few nights, as our plan was to live again in the apartment above our sundries store. We would have to paint, make small repairs and then set about the task of becoming reacquainted with the community. A daunting task if ever there was one! I shall never forget how hopeful Adam was—how sure he was that everything would be okay.

For my part, I was as nervous as a cat in a room full of rocking chairs! Besides the change in scenery, I faced the prospect of navigating the social community knowing the truth about my own parentage. I had to find my own solicitor, present my letter and proceed with claiming my inheritance. I didn't know Claudette Page, but what woman would want to hear the news that her brother had had a child out of wedlock—two, if you included my missing sister—who would be the heir to the fortune she thought she had inherited? As Adam tended to his legal affairs, I tended to mine. I found a lawyer named Mr. Peyton on Royal Street, not too far from our shop. With some surprise, he listened to my story and read the letter.

"How amazing! To think, I knew the man and never knew that he…well, I never knew he had a daughter."

"Two daughters. He has two daughters, Mr. Peyton."

"Well, technically, just one living heir. Calpurnia Cottonwood was declared dead years ago. Her inheritance from her mother was claimed by her father, or the man we believed was her father. How incredible!" He twisted his waxed mustache tips and stared with wide eyes. "I suppose you have something that would corroborate your story. A will, perhaps, or some other documentation."

The question surprised me. I had not expected that I would need to prove my identity. I confessed as much to the attorney.

"Let me speak frankly to you, my dear. This is quite a thing to present to a judge. He may not believe that this letter is from Dr. Page or that it is a true document. I am almost certain that before we proceed, we need something else. At least something that we can use to authenticate the handwriting."

"What? Who would make up such a thing? I would never…"

"I believe you. I am on your side, and I want you to have what belongs to you, but…well…have you met Claudette Page? Dr. Page's sister?"

"No, I haven't."

"There is no way that lady is going to lie down for this. Not for one minute! I have never met such an independent-minded woman, and she is most disagreeable. To top it all off, you'll be accusing her brother of a great lapse in virtue, a topic that is particularly important to the lady. She is one of our city's strongest advocates for 'greater Christian morality,' as she calls it. I heard a rumor—it can't be true, though—that even the local pastors consult her before they preach their sermons. Apparently, they were becoming too liberal here for her liking."

"She must be very influential to hold such sway over the community." I fiddled with my gloves, unsure what to do next. How could the man who claimed to be my father do this to me?

"Still, if Hoyt—I mean, Dr. Page—took the trouble to send you this letter, then chances are he made some record of it somewhere. I'll check with the courthouse to see if there is anything useful there. My friend Mr. Schumacher is the director of our bank. I can inquire with him about any accounts or safety deposit boxes. If we cannot produce supporting documents, we will have no choice but to meet with Miss Page personally. I am sure she would want to avoid a scandal, so that should work in our favor."

"I don't wish to cause a scandal, and I'm not here to take anything that's not mine, Mr. Peyton. I confess I am just as surprised about all this as anyone else is." I paused and then asked the question I was dying to ask. "What do you know about my mother and sister?"

"Until today, I would have sworn that Christine Beaumont was a saint. Never had a bad word to say about anyone, and she lived with the devil himself! I don't blame her too harshly for wanting to find some happiness in this world outside that cold fish of a husband. However, as your attorney, I advise you to keep that letter to yourself. No one, not even Miss Page, needs to read Hoyt's confession."

"I will keep it to myself." He rose to see me out, but I had one more question. "What about Calpurnia? What can you tell me about her?"

"I didn't know her personally, but I did attend her coming-out party. My son Gerald was quite taken with her, but unfortunately for him, she showed no interest. I do remember she was very shy, some might even say bookish, but still a lovely young woman. You look very much like her. Yes, if anyone saw you, they might look twice. That might help your case, Miss Iverson— I mean, Miss Page."

I rose to my feet smiling. I liked the sound of my true name. "I will leave this to you then, Mr. Peyton. My brother and I are staying at the Iverson Sundries Store."

"Oh yes! I'll be in touch soon."

I walked back to the store and set about cleaning the place. What would my parents think about all this? I tried not to think about it. Maybe it was best that I gave it up—left the name behind and spent the rest of my days as an Iverson. It was certainly something I needed to think about. As I swept up the dust, thinking and stewing over the fact that Adam was gone yet again, a shadow darkened my doorway. A woman dressed in black from head to toe blocked the sunlight, her tall, lace-lined bonnet adding height to her already imposing figure. I raised a hand to my eyes and *asked, "May I help you, madam? Our store isn't open yet, but if you'd like to place an order for something specific…"*

She walked in and untied the bow under her chin. With an unimpressed expression, she looked around the store and then finally at me. "Delilah Iverson, I presume?"

"Yes. May I help you?" I smiled at the sunlit figure.

"I was just getting to know your brother at the carpentry shop. We haven't been properly introduced. My name is Claudette—Claudette Page." She didn't offer me a hand of friendship or even a smile. She held her bonnet to her as if she were afraid that the dust might soil her hat beyond repair. As she stepped out of the light, I could see her features more clearly now. She had pale skin, carefully curled black hair and full lips. I imagined at one time she had been an attractive woman but never one prone to smiling.

"Miss Page, nice to meet you. May I help you?"

"Are you or are you not Delilah Iverson?" So the swords were sharpening, were they? Miss Page did not know me if she thought I would be cowed by her unfriendly attitude. I knew who she was but not why she was here.

"That depends on who you ask, Miss Page."

"You have the look of your mother," she said as she stared around the room at the crates and boxes.

I didn't know what to say. Who was I to argue with such an observation? I had never laid eyes on my mother. I felt my chin rise and I clung to my broom handle, fighting the urge to hit her with it repeatedly. "The nature of your visit confuses me, Miss Page."

"Oh, I just wanted to have a look around."

"I see," I said.

"You know, I wrote to your brother while you were in Canada. I offered to buy this place so you wouldn't have to come all this way. I mean, the economy here isn't what it used to be. You might find it difficult to turn a profit, Miss Iverson. Mobile already has a sundries shop. Do we really need two?"

"A little competition is good for the economy, at least that's what I've read. Do you have a different theory?"

"Yes, I have a theory. I think you're an opportunist, Miss Iverson. Your coward brother ran from the war, and now the two of you are back to exploit the hardworking people of Mobile. But I won't let you do that!"

"How dare you talk about my brother in such an offensive manner! My brother is no coward!"

"So you see how it is then." Her voice was like sharpened steel. "I care for my brother as you care for yours. Why sully Hoyt's name now that he's gone, now that he's dead. Let sleeping dogs lie, Miss Iverson, and I'll do the same for you."

"Are you threatening me, Miss Page?"

Another shadow appeared in the back door. It was Adam!

"Come now. Do I need to threaten such a sensible girl as yourself? Lay down your claim to my brother, and I will do the same for yours."

Adam walked into the shop from the stockroom, shock written all over his face. "What? What claim are you referring to, Miss Page?"

"Isn't it interesting that when the war came to our fair city, you were nowhere to be found?" Adam's face turned beet red, and he walked to the half-open door and held it open. "If Miss Iverson leaves her ridiculous claim at the courthouse door, I will keep my opinions to myself. No one has to know that you were a coward, Adam."

"How dare you!" My voice rose in anger. "Get out of my store! I will make no such promise! Who do you think you are that you can come here and threaten me—threaten us? Get out!" She stomped out, leaving us alone. I turned to Adam, but the damage was already done.

All his hopes were dashed now—his male Norwegian pride crushed like flowers under a bootheel. His worst fears were realized. The gossip had begun—Adam Iverson was a coward. Adam Iverson was yellow. I could hear his imagination at work already.

"Adam!" I called after him, but I didn't see him until late that evening. And so it was for two weeks until I heard again from my attorney…

I forced myself to close the small, worn book. I didn't have time to focus on another mystery like what happened to Delilah Iverson. Detra Ann was fighting for her life, and the gravity of the situation became very real to me. I needed to help my friend.

Finally, I knew how I could do it.

Chapter Sixteen

Cynthia Dowd walked out of the tiny hospital bathroom and gasped.

"Oh, I'm sorry. I didn't mean to startle you. How is she?"

With a worried expression, she glanced at her comatose daughter and whispered, "I think she's doing better. See, she's got color in her cheeks this evening. I think she knows we are here, don't you?"

I politely agreed with her and followed her back to Detra Ann's bedside. I sat in the noisy pleather seat and tried to be quiet. I needed Cynthia to leave—this would be dangerous, but I had to do it. Making contact with Detra Ann could only help. At least that's what I believed. Since Cynthia was whispering, I whispered to her, "Have you seen Ashland and TD?"

"Yes, they went to grab a bite to eat. Ashland told me he wanted to bring you something too. You must have just missed him. They went to Jumpers for takeout. They'll be back soon."

"What about you, Cynthia? Don't you need to eat something?"

"No, I can't eat. Not while she's like this."

I sighed. "Yes, I can see that." I sat quietly again, trying to work out how I could get her out of here. I needed to be alone with Detra Ann, and I needed enough time to fall asleep and make contact with her. I prayed that I wasn't making a terrible mistake by attempting this.

She leaned back in the seat beside me and said with a smile, "Wasn't it nice that the ladies came to see me this morning?"

"Yes, very nice indeed. Bette seems to truly care about you." Bette! As discreetly as I could I reached for my phone and texted her while Cynthia sat staring at her daughter.

Bette, this is Nancy Drew. I need your help. Can you come to the hospital? I need to get Cynthia out of the room.

My "Nancy Drew" reference was an observation that Detective Simmons had made about Bette and me during the Mia incident. She'd called us Angela Lansbury and Nancy Drew. It had tickled Bette tremendously.

On the way. What do you have in mind?

Can't share now but it's crucial. Please help.

Roger that.

Bette added a smiley face and I tapped one back. For the next fifteen minutes, I chitchatted with Cynthia as she talked about Detra Ann's last beauty pageant, how she'd shocked the committee by performing "Dixie" on her flute while leading her white poodle through an obstacle course. It was quite humorous to hear, and I was sure that Detra Ann would be mortified that her mother would tell such childhood secrets.

The door opened, but it wasn't Bette. Ashland and TD were back with food. "There you are," Ashland said.

"What's up with not answering your phone?" I checked it and noticed his two messages.

"Oops, sorry. I don't know how I missed those," I whispered.

"Why are we whispering?" Ashland asked me, but it was Cynthia who answered.

"Because she's asleep. She'll wake up when she's ready. Now you boys go out in the hall and let her rest a while."

"Hey, everybody!" Bette missed the speech about whispering, but Cynthia didn't say a word to her. "How is our princess doing, Cynthia? Oh, look at her. I think I see color in those pretty cheeks. I'd say she's on the mend. Have the doctors come in recently?"

"They won't be in until morning."

"You know what? You don't look so hot, Cynthia. I mean, you look pale, darling." I loved the way Bette said "darling." It was the long drawn out version, "daw-lin." It just kind of lingered there.

"I don't care what I look like right now."

"I'm not talking about your gorgeous face, Cynth. You can't neglect your health right now. Not when Detra Ann is going to need you so much. When was the last time you had some fresh air?"

"I don't know. This morning, maybe?"

"I tell you what, let's go for a walk. Maybe visit the gift shop and find her some flowers. She'll like seeing those when she wakes up."

"No, Bette! I can't leave her. What happens if she wakes up and I'm not here?"

"You won't be gone long, and Carrie Jo is here. You can trust her to stay, right?"

"Oh, yes, ma'am. I'll stay. Ashland brought me some food, and I have a pillow and blanket. Take all the time you want."

"I won't be gone long, though," Cynthia said, stretching her back before she walked over to the mirror. She stared at herself disapprovingly. I felt bad for manipulating her, but I needed her to leave. Ashland watched the whole thing quietly and didn't interfere, but he knew something was up. I'd have to explain what I was doing. That would be tricky.

Bette kept her game face on as they left and didn't give a clue that I had called her. Now that was a true friend. I would have to thank her somehow later.

"What's up, beautiful? You're up to something. You might as well tell me now."

"Yes, I am up to something." I arranged the pillow and blanket in the chair next to Detra Ann. I reached over and held her hand lovingly. Through tear-filled eyes, I stared at her perfect pink manicured nails. She'd tried to help me, to save me from something in my house— probably Isla—and now she was trapped, trapped in another world. I had to go help her. Suddenly awareness crept across Ashland's face.

"No, Carrie Jo. This isn't a good idea! What happens if you make contact with her and then you're in a coma too?"

TD broke in, "Wait! Ashland's right. Detra Ann wouldn't want that."

"I have my friend's hand, that's all. I'm tired and am going to take a nap now. If I see her, I will talk to her, maybe get her to come back to us."

"You can do that?" TD sounded unsure but willing to give it a shot if it brought Detra Ann back to him.

"I've never done it before, TD, but I would like to try. With all my heart I will try. She loves you so much. I can't imagine that she'd want to be too far away from you."

"Ashland, I don't want to put her in danger, but if she can find her..."

"I know. Okay, Carrie Jo. I guess it's okay, not that you needed my permission. I know you. You would have done it anyway."

"I sure would have. Now turn out the light, please, and try to keep the nurses occupied for the next thirty minutes."

"Sure, but I am going to be right outside. If I hear something, I am coming in."

"Fair enough."

Ashland turned off the light and held onto the doorknob for a minute. I smiled at him to reassure him and then closed my eyes. Sleep didn't come immediately; there were too many distractions. To make matters worse, I could hear Henri's deep, booming voice in the hallway. He'd come! But I had to focus on Detra Ann.

Detra Ann, where are you? Why won't you come back to us?

I rubbed her hand gently, just like my mother would do for me when I was sick as a child, before she became sick herself. It had always comforted me; hopefully it would help me make a connection with Detra Ann.

All of a sudden, I stepped out of reality and into the dream world, and what I saw terrified me. I wasn't holding the hand of beautiful, tanned Detra Ann—I was holding the hand of Christine Beaumont!

I looked down at Christine, only I wasn't a character in a dream or some ghost from the past—I was me! Wrapped around her arms and legs were black snake-like cords that held her in place. "Help me! They won't let me go!" I stared, but only for a moment. A disturbing sound from the hallway, like a demonic train, shook the building and threatened to bust through the wall. I began to furiously untie the cords and free her from the hospital bed. At first, I didn't think I could release her, but suddenly the cords fell off. She sat up in the bed and put her arms around me.

"You can see me! You have to help me! He won't let me go! Where is Hoyt? Hurry!"

With frightened fingers I untied the last tie. "I will help you, Christine—but where is my friend, Detra Ann? I have to know!" The crashing train noise ceased, and suddenly the room became foggy so quickly that I could barely see Christine. But I didn't release her hand, and she clung to mine. She slid off the bed, her full skirts rustling as she did. The gray fog cleared and she stared at me, then recognition crossed her face. She squeezed my hand even tighter—I thought she would hug me again.

"I don't understand how you are here, my own dearest. How I have missed you! Please help me! Oh no! They're here, Calpurnia—run!" she sobbed. Her brow beaded with sweat, and her dark blond hair became wet with it.

I pulled on her hand. "I'm not Calpurnia. I'm Carrie Jo. What about Detra Ann? Where is she?"

"We have to go now, Isla is coming—my tormentor, the one who tied me here!" The door blew open, and the sound of a thousand angry invisible bees filled the room. It was the same sound I'd heard in the Moonlight Garden the night Ashland, TD and I defeated Isla—or thought we had.

"Christine! Where are you going? I've only just begun to play with you. So happy that Calpurnia could join us," Isla purred, her perfect blond ringlets bouncing against her cherubic cheeks.

"I'm not Calpurnia!" I shouted, but who was going to hear me over the furious noise? Christine tugged on my hand, and we ran pell-mell down the hallway to the back wall. I screamed, preparing for the pain of running into the wall, but nothing happened. Instead I opened my eyes to find myself and Christine standing in the ballroom of Seven Sisters.

A lone candelabrum provided light in the dreary blackness that surrounded us. Catching my breath—I thankfully still had breath—I noticed a figure walking toward us. It was Jeremiah Cottonwood. He wore all black except for shiny silver coat buttons that glittered in the dimness. He looked as if he were going to a funeral, and then it occurred to me that this was how he must have been dressed for his own funeral. Hoyt Page had killed him over a hundred and fifty years ago.

"Christine, daughter…how nice of you to come to my party. More guests will be arriving soon. Come closer and embrace me." He stretched out his arms to us with a devilish smile, and I noticed that the tiny silver buttons weren't buttons at all but spiders that fell off his velvet suit and scrambled across the hardwood floor. I shuddered at the sight.

"Stay away from us, Jeremiah."

His evil smile vanished, his mouth opened and an unearthly scream rose—it penetrated my very bones. "I'm alive! I'm still alive," I kept telling myself. I hoped it was true. How could I be here?

Still, Christine squeezed my hand. "We have each other now, Calpurnia, and nothing will stop us from going to our peace. Nothing! Step aside, Jeremiah! Your curse has been broken."

He did not move but stared at us, his neck bent down, his head tilted up. The evil smile had returned, and his dark eyes shimmered strangely. He observed us like an animal would, an animal stalking its prey.

Fearlessly, Christine continued. She walked around him with sure steps, never letting go of my hand. "Remember the words you whispered in my ear the night you killed me? You cursed me. You said no one would ever love me again, not now and not for eternity." She stepped toward him bravely, ignoring his angry, purple face and the beastly, guttural sounds he made. "You are a liar! I am loved!"

"I loved you!"

She smiled at him. "Yes, I remember how you loved me, Jeremiah. I remember how you slid the rope around my neck. I remember how you tightened it and raised me from the ground until I swung higher and higher. Oh yes, I remember your love! You exacted your revenge and stole my life, and now you think you can keep me in death too? What justice is that? I will be free!"

"What do you know of love, Christine?" He hissed at her.

"You condemned me and then killed me, but what you didn't know was that you set me free. Free from you who cannot love!"

"Don't speak to me about love, harlot!"

"Call me what you will, but I have love. My daughter loves me! The power of our love breaks your curse, Jeremiah!"

"But I'm not..." I started to explain myself, but then the invisible bees began to circle me again. It was Isla, here to serve Jeremiah, to see to it that he exacted his revenge on us for all eternity. Briefly I wondered what debt she was paying by serving him in death, for I knew in life she cared nothing for him. He had been amusing to her and, like most men, a means to whatever end she imagined or schemed.

"What kind of fool do you take me for, Christine? This is not Calpurnia, your bastard daughter."

Suddenly, Jeremiah reached for Christine with a gnarled hand and snatched her viciously from my grip with such force that I fell backward. He slid his arm around her neck. The look of fear had returned to her face, and I could see her surprise. She'd failed. How could she have confused me for Calpurnia?

Whatever the reason, I had failed Christine. And I had failed Detra Ann.

"This can't be," she yelled. "Calpurnia?"

"You are mine, Christine! And now another has come to join our party! Bring in our guest, Isla." Isla stepped out of the outer darkness and with a wave of her hands made candlelight appear around the room—it looked just as it had the night of her coming-out party. Wax candles burned bright, an orchestra played in the corner of the room and black-clad dancers took their places on the floor. My skin felt cold and clammy, as if death were nearby. It was, wasn't it? She wore a purple dress with white ribbons at the sleeves, and her invisible hemline never touched the ground.

I couldn't be here! I couldn't be! How is this even possible?

"Hoyt!" I heard Christine scream with all her might. "Hoyt! Help me, my love!"

I swung my head to the door and wanted to run to him but couldn't get up. I suddenly felt heavy, as if my limbs were covered with concrete. I couldn't move or get up—only helplessly watch whatever was about to happen. *Oh my God! That's TD! Why can't she see it's Terrence Dale and not Hoyt Page?*

"I'm here, Christine." Then, TD wasn't TD anymore. He was taller, thinner with darker hair, and he wore a tailored brown suit. "I failed you before, but I will not fail you now, my love. Come to me. Let her go, Cottonwood. You have no claim on her."

She wrangled free from Jeremiah but only for a second. Grinning, Cottonwood slid his arm around her neck again and said savagely, "She's mine, Page. She always will be mine. You may have her heart, but I have a covenant that cannot be broken, the covenant of marriage. I am on the side of right."

Hoyt stormed toward Jeremiah, determined to rescue Christine, but he ran into the invisible force that Isla seemed to manipulate so easily with just her hands.

"Isla! Stop this! How can you let him use you like this?" I pleaded with her. I was desperate.

She giggled and pressed her hands together, a move that forced me almost flat to the hardwood floor.

"How can you set her free, Page? See, she is mine still."

"You are a murderer! You murdered Christine. You are an unjust man, and you have no right to keep her here! You would have killed our daughter too, if I had allowed it. I saved her, Christine. I saved Delilah!"

"Let me go, Jeremiah. Please I beg you." Christine struggled less now, and I could see that she was giving up. "Don't keep me here anymore. I can't bear it. I want to be with Hoyt and my children."

"Did you think that I didn't know about you and Hoyt, about your bastard children—the ones you tried to pass off as mine? What a fine game player you were, dear! Granted it took me years to discover that Calpurnia was his ill-begotten stock, but once I knew, everything changed. You stole that from me! I will never let you leave, not now—not ever!"

"Christine! Christine! Come to me now! Please! Before it's too late!" Hoyt cried out from his knees. Isla whirled around us, and this time she sailed by so close that I could smell honeysuckle and something else…death. I could feel her excitement as she waited to kill me.

"I can't, he won't let me go! It's no use, Hoyt," Christine cried pitifully. For a second, her face faded—I could plainly see Detra Ann! Jeremiah was holding Detra Ann!

"Fight, Detra Ann! Fight!" My friend struggled with renewed vigor, but it lasted only a few seconds.

Isla growled, but I continued to shout, "Fight! You are not Christine, you are Detra Ann Dowd. You are my friend, and I care about you! Now fight, damn it!"

Jeremiah seemed confused, but then Detra Ann's face disappeared and it was just Christine again, crying hopelessly.

"Let her go, Jeremiah! She's not Christine!" Finally, I could stand. I reached for Hoyt and helped him up too. A swell of terrible music rose in the ballroom, and the once-frozen dancers began to dance around us. The stale air moved like a brewing storm.

"You are a guest in my house now, my dear. Please join the dance," Jeremiah said, squeezing Detra Ann's neck, choking the life from her.

"NO! Detra Ann! TD, do something!" I screamed as a faceless man in a black suit whipped his arm around my waist and spun me about, lifting me a few feet from the ground. We danced in a circle, his invisible hand on my waist, pulling me tighter and tighter.

"Calpurnia, my darling," he whispered. I recognized that voice! David Garrett! He was here too, trapped with everyone else! It took everything I had not to scream my head off as I struggled between my fear of falling to the ground and my terror at being held by this faceless ghoul.

The doors opened again, and the dancers froze to see who else had arrived. It was Bette!

I gasped and then screamed at the top of my lungs, "Bette! Run! Leave before it's too late!" But she didn't appear to hear me. The ghost that held me swirled us back to the ground, and I violently pushed away from him. I made my way through the dancers—I had to get to Bette!

"Let her go!" she commanded Jeremiah. "Now!" Bette stepped toward Christine as he visibly released his hold on her. Then the oddest thing happened—Bette transformed before my very eyes. Her perfect puffs of white curls grew, and her hair darkened to a lustrous dark brown. She appeared tall and thin, like Hoyt. In a flash, her blue capris with the yellow daisies all over were replaced with a flowing pink and white gown and a lovely white hat with a soft ivory-colored feather. She walked toward the center of the room and stood between Hoyt and Jeremiah. The bees went silent, and I noticed that even Isla slid as far away from Bette as she could. Fear, which had been tangible and sovereign just moments ago, fled into the shadows like a wild animal along with Isla and her cohorts. Peace filled the room. I alone stood out from the darkness. Hoyt (or TD, I wasn't sure which) was only a few feet away from me. He watched with a rapt expression of pure love.

Bette wasn't Bette. She was young and beautiful—she was Delilah Iverson.

"Can it be?" Christine's hand flew to her chest, and she took a step away from Jeremiah. He did not reach for her again. I noticed that he too had retreated a little.

"Yes, Mother. I am Delilah, your daughter. I am here to take you home."

In one bold move, Christine covered the distance between them and embraced her tightly. After a moment, Delilah stepped away, touching her arm as she walked toward Jeremiah. His typical haughty expression had vanished, replaced with a look of abject despair and anger.

"My mother doesn't belong to you anymore. You were wrong—she is loved. I love her, just as my sister loves her. We are leaving here now, Jeremiah Cottonwood, and don't think to stop us."

He backed away as a light surrounded her. I couldn't explain it, but love shone through her like a big bright candle. No. Like a star.

Arm in arm, they walked toward the outside door. Another light, brighter and bigger than even Delilah, shone brilliantly. As the door swung open, that light filled the ballroom in a flash.

Hoyt stumbled after them, pleading, "You can't leave me again, Christine. I love you and always will. Don't leave me now."

Christine paused on the garden path and gave him a beautiful smile. She reached out her hand, and he ran to her.

"Wait! TD! You can't go!" I cried out, unsure what to think about what was happening. I watched their glowing figures walk through the Moonlight Garden, Delilah on the right, Hoyt on the left and Christine in the middle. I didn't dare take my eyes off of them, but I could "feel" the others around me disappearing into nothingness.

Instead of giggling, I heard Isla crying. Crying that her life and afterlife were now completely over. She would go down into the grave and be gone forever.

Worm food now, I suppose...

Jeremiah didn't whimper or wail, but simply slid into a small black hole that appeared in the floor. He didn't even make a sound as he slipped away down into the abyss. The hole closed, leaving only a small scorch mark on the floor.

I looked back up and saw the three lights, Delilah, Christine and Hoyt, fading away into the dark night. They were together at last. I wondered if they would simply go to sleep or if they would have time, their time—the time that was stolen from them. I didn't know. I hoped they found Calpurnia waiting wherever they were going.

I sat on the hardwood floor and cried my eyes out.

Epilogue

Ashland and Carrie Jo stepped out onto the dais and faced the excited crowd. It was springtime in Mobile, bright and cool—the perfect day for unveiling the new Bette Marshall Museum and the Terrence Dale House. The new museum housed the extension of the Seven Sisters art collection, while the Dale House was the rebuilt slave quarters, reconstructed according to TD's plans. It had been next on his list after restoring the Moonlight Garden. Ashland and TD had wanted to restore the plantation to be as historically accurate as they could make it, and this addition would do just that. Carrie Jo had commissioned a painting of Muncie that now hung in the foyer of the Marshall Museum. It was one of my favorite places to visit.

I wondered what our missing friends would think about the honors we bestowed upon them today. I wondered if TD remembered me—I liked to imagine that he did. I thought about him every day. At first, he was all I could think about. How could he have simply walked out of the hospital and disappeared? But slowly, the space between the crashing waves of grief grew, and eventually I found the strength to continue. But my future was forever changed by his absence.

Ashland made his speech, and the crowd applauded. I watched Carrie Jo as she stood smiling by his side. Funny how close we were now. She was like the sister I never had. I couldn't imagine life without her, and I would forever be in her debt for what she did.

"But none of this would be possible without the help of Detra Ann Dowd, the director of the Seven Sisters

Living Museum. Please make her welcome." The crowd again applauded, and I solemnly took the podium. I closed my eyes for a second and let the sunlight beam down on me. We'd worked like dogs to make this happen in such a short time, but at least it was done. These weren't just important landmarks and museums. They were memorials to our friends.

It was the least we could do.

According to the papers, Bette Marshall had died of a sudden heart attack in her home. TD had simply disappeared. For a while, rumors circulated that he'd fallen off the wagon again, but when he didn't reappear, everyone changed their mind. I knew the truth. So did Ashland, Henri and Carrie Jo. That was all that mattered.

"Thank you, everyone, for your support throughout this process. Special thanks to the Historical Society for your tireless commitment to Seven Sisters…." I read my notes and tried to keep a smile in my voice. I thought I did okay. When my speech was finished, I took a seat on the dais. Carrie Jo reached for my hand and squeezed it. Suddenly, I missed TD so badly that I almost cried. I squeezed her hand back, and she didn't let go. I was glad for that.

When the ceremony ended, we stepped off the dais and I fell into Henri's big arms. He'd become a dear friend to me these past six months. I was glad that he had decided to move back to Mobile. Within a month, he'd purchased the Cotton City Antique Store, and I'd spent a bit of time there helping him set up his displays. It was peaceful work, and he seemed to value my opinion.

Despite what some of the wagging tongues might think, we weren't romantically involved. But I cared deeply for him.

We spent the next thirty minutes greeting visitors and answering questions. When it was over, I gave a sigh of relief. I was leaving Seven Sisters at the end of the month. My assistant, Rachel Kowalski, was taking over the directorship. I knew I was leaving the house in good hands. Of that, I had no worries. I'd given enough to the house. We all had.

It was time to leave the past behind…time to say goodbye to Seven Sisters. I took a walk through the Moonlight Garden. I touched the flowers and breathed in the scent of magnolias and roses. I picked a few petals off the ground and walked to the Atlas fountain.

"Goodbye, TD." I tossed the petals into the water and watched them spin wildly and then slowly sink to the bottom.

I turned my face to the sun once more and felt peace wash over me. I couldn't say for sure, but in that moment I believed he heard me.

For the last time, I walked out of the maze and back to the house. Henri, Ashland and Carrie Jo waited for me. We walked through the house and closed the door behind us.

We didn't look back.

Read more from M.L. Bullock

The Seven Sisters Series

Seven Sisters
Moonlight Falls on Seven Sisters
Shadows Stir at Seven Sisters
The Stars that Fell
The Stars We Walked Upon
The Sun Rises Over Seven Sisters

The Desert Queen Series

The Tale of Nefret
The Falcon Rises
The Kingdom of Nefertiti
The Song of the Bee-Eater (forthcoming)

The Sugar Hill Series (forthcoming)

Wife of the Left Hand
Fire on the Ramparts
Blood by Candlelight

The Sirens Gate Series

The Mermaid's Gift
The Blood Feud (forthcoming)
The Wrath of Minerva (forthcoming)
The Lorelei Curse (forthcoming)
The Fortunate Star (forthcoming)

The Southern Gothic Series

Being with Beau

To receive updates on her latest releases,
visit her website at MLBullock.com
and subscribe to her mailing list.

Made in the USA
Lexington, KY
01 November 2016